Coon Dogs and Outhouses

Volume 2

Tall Tales

From The Mississippi Delta

Luke Boyd

This Book is Sponsored by TotalRecall Publications, Inc.
1103 Middlecreek
Friendswood, Texas 77546
281-992-3131 281-482-5390 Fax

Worldwide Book and eBook publication and distribution by: TotalRecall Publications.

Printed in United States of America

Printed and bound by Lightning Source, Inc. in the USA and UK

Paper Back

ISBN: 978-1-59095-839-1

UPC 6-43977-5839-5

eBook: Adobe Acrobat

ISBN 978-1-59095-840-7

UPC 6-43977-5840-1

The sponsoring editor is Bruce Moran and the production supervisor is Corby R. Tate.

For Kimberly and David

The Next Generation

About the Author

Dr. Lucas G. "Luke" Boyd first saw the light of day in a three-room shotgun house on Jabe Dunaway's place near Anguilla, Mississippi. It was the depths of the Depression. His father had lost everything and had returned to the land to feed his family. However, within a few years he was managing one of those sprawling, 2,000-plus acre cotton plantations the Delta was know8 for. This plantation culture of his early years left an indelible mark on young Luke.

A stroke of good fortune and a good scholarship allowed him to attend The University of Mississippi, where he earned a B.S. degree. During his career he attended a total of five universities, three of which saw fit to grant him degrees: Middle Tennessee State University (M.S.), The University of Tennessee (Ph.D. in English History). Stints at The University of North Carolina and The University of Chattanooga were for special study in Economics and Far Eastern History, respectively.

He entered the Army through the ROTC program and served for two years as a lst Lt. in an armored unit.

After leaving the service, he began a career in education which spanned 43 years both at the secondary and college levels. He retired after serving for 19 years as Principal of Battle Ground Academy, a private, college preparatory school in Franklin, Tennessee.

His publishing credits include: two books, Coon Dogs and Outhouses, Vol. I, Don't Call Me Hero (ghost writer) the story of a WW II bomber pilot; 9 short stores; l article in The Tennessee Encyclopedia of History and Culture. He currently writes regular columns for a local newspaper, The

Williamson Herald, and for Mature Lifestyles magazine.

He and his wife, Sara, have been married for 53 years and have two children and two grandchildren. They live in Franklin, Tennessee.

About the Book

Sometimes I stop and try to figure out where the stories come from and why I write the way I do. I'm sure much of it is a result of the land I grew up on and the people who were trying to scratch a living from it. One of my earliest memories is of a large fire in the middle of the cotton field. It was wintertime and I was helping Daddy burn chunks of stumps and roots which had accumulated during the crop season. It was a new ground farm only recently drained and released from the clutches of the brackish water of a Mississippi bayou. The soil was buckshot - rich, black, and grainy – unlike the light-colored, sandy loam of the old Delta. But the type of soil doesn't matter. If he stays in contact with it long enough, the land will brand a man as surely as the red-hot iron brands a Western calf. I'm sure the flat, almost treeless, bayou studded Delta of my early years which later was replaced by Mississippi's rolling, red-clay hills both placed their marks on me. My family had long been people of the soil and although I chose another profession, I have always been aware of the pull of the land.

And then, there were the people—those quirky, down-to-earth folk who saw the world and their place in it through a different set of lens. My family tree had plenty of these sitting on all the branches and there were plenty more just down the road or over the hill. And in our rural society, they could not hide. Everyone knew them and also knew all about them. And the stories of their quirky escapades and misadventures were told and retold until they took on a life of their own. For, you see, that's the way the common history was kept alive and where much of our entertainment came from—through the stories.

It was the Depression and very few areas were as economically depressed as the rural South. The road in front of our house was dirt (mud when it rained) and with no electric lights and no plumbing, we lived a bare and stark existence. There was no money to purchase entertainment so we made our own. Whether rocking on the front porch before bedtime or sitting around the kitchen table after supper, it was story time. Daddy was a storyteller and had a number of tales he told on a regular basis. My brother and I enjoyed new stuff but if talk got slow, we'd ask to hear about "the kicking gun" or "The Stone Mountain deer." These and more of his tales are included in Coon Dogs, Volume I.

Stories flew thick and fast when visitors were in the house. With my uncles it was tales about the family or about people they grew up with. With neighbors I learned who had been caught making moonshine and who was stepping out on his wife. Much of my early education came from sitting on the floor off to the side during these sessions. I not only learned the stories, I also learned how to tell one.

This Coon Dogs Volume II of is a little different from Coon Dogs Volume I. Most of these pieces are short stories but many of them came from some of these early tales. Most contain some element of truth although sometime that element is pretty small. Some are almost totally true. Hopefully, the reader will have a difficult time distinguishing between what is fact and what is fiction. Just where the reader draws the line is immaterial. The important question is: "Do they entertain?" I hope I have extended the front porch or added chairs around the kitchen table.

Although this volume does not contain actual stories about a coon dog or an outhouse, they are there in the background. Both are always close to any rural, Southern setting. And most of these stories are about those rural, Southern folk who are really a breed unto themselves. For, you see, those are the folk I really know—the people of the soil. That's why I considered myself a "Southern writer" which my wife, Sara, defines as "someone who writes about nothing but still makes it interesting." There's more truth in that statement than most of us are willing to admit.

Even though the words and stories are mine, I owe a tremendous debt to others who actually made them come to print. Foremost was Sara, my "tech support," who did all the typing and computer work. Our marriage has survived for 53 years, three books, and numerous short literary pieces—a remarkable feat in and of itself. Thanks also to Steve "Hog" Reeves who was in the right place at the right time and who has his own story to tell. And last, but surely not least, thanks to Bruce Moran and the folks at TotalRecall Publications who know how to put it all together.

Table of Contents

01
THE DAY THE HOGS GOT LOOSE

I's a-tellin' you whut's the gospel truth, I ain't never gonna git myself involved ever again with Press-tone Murphy and nonna his projects. Why, that man could screw up a one-car funeral and everbody knows it. And I knows it. Hit beats me why I don't jest leave him be. Well, come to think of hit, hit don't really beat me. I knows why. Ol' Press-tone is a generous sort. Whether hit's a woman or a jug a-shine, he's a-willin' to share. Sometimes both at the same time.

Anyways, I wuz by Press-tone's place last Saddy a-settin' on his front porch. He has a artificial, potted tree there 'tween two rockers. Thas whur he keeps his shine there a-settin' in the pot when he has any which he usually does. We wuz a passin' the jug twixt us an' a-talkin' when he sez to me, he sez, "I needs you ta hep me fer a little spell this comin' Tuesday."

"Watch yer gonna do?" I sez back.

He sez, "You see them hogs out thar in the lot?"

A-course I could see them hogs and I could smell 'em better'n I could see 'em, so I sez, "Yep."

And he sez ta me, he sez, "I needs ta haul most of 'em into Milton to the livestock auction and I needs somebody ta hep me."

I sez, "Why don't ya git a-holt of ole Benny Gee? He's gotta livestock truck and he hauls animals all over the county fer everbody?"

"He charges too much," he sez back. "And he wants to take 'em on Monday which means I'll hafta pay a pen and boarding fee to the barn plus the commission fer sellin' 'em. What I aim to do is ta haul 'em down thar myself and jes back up to the gate and run 'em through the auction. That way all I'll hafta pay is the commission. I raised them hogs and I don't see no reason ta be a-givin' ma profits away ta other folks."

"That sounds like a good idea," I sez.

"Hit is. Hit is a good idea and it come outa this jug a-shine," he sez. "I wuz jest a-settin' here yestiddy and a-drinkin' on the first part of hit and the idea jest come to me. And the more I drunk, the better the idea got. Why, hit ain't nothin' like a good jug a-shine ta give a feller ideas. And there ain't no tellin' what kinda ideas they is in this bottom part."

I sez ta him, I sez, "Watch yer gonna haul 'em in? We can't git 'em in the bed of yore pickup."

"That trailer rat over thar," he sez.

"That's jest a two-wheel, flat bed trailer," I sez. "Hit don't have no sides. You know them hogs ain't gonna jest stand there on it whilst you drive 'em down the road."

And he sez to me, he sez, "That's where the shine come in. Hits done give me the idea on what ta do. You just show up Tuesday morning and I'll be ready fer ya."

I said I would and we rocked and finished the shine. Thar wasn't no more ideas in it though.

Well, I showed up this mornin' and Press-tone wuz ready. He had done taken some scrap lumber and some plyboard and built little sides around that trailer. He had the hogs separated out, too, with the one's we 'uz a-takin' in the near lot. "How many is we a-takin'?" I sez.

He sez, "13." And I stopped and give 'em a funny look. "Wot's wrong?" he sez.

And I sez to 'im, "I don't like to be a-foolin' with nothing that adds up to 13. Couldn't you jest leave one or add another one?"

"Naw, I can't," he sez. "I'm a –keepin' my breedin' stock and these here is what I wanna sell. 13 is jest a number like any other number."

"No, hit ain't," I sez. "Hit's the devil's number and is to be avoided. But since I done tol' you I'd hep, I's gonna hep but I don't feel easy about it."

Then Press-tone backed that trailer up to the lot gate and let the tailgate down. We opened the gate and left it a-stickin' straight out. Press-tone said it would give us somethin' to run the hogs up against and hep direct them onto the trailer. Hit worked jest like Press-tone said. We'd run some around the lot fence and when they'd come to that gate a-stickin' out, they'd jest swerve on up onto the trailer. After we'd got seven up thar, we took two pieces of plyboard 'bout three foot high and pushed the hogs up to the front part of the trailer. Then Press-tone got a hammer and some nails and nailed through the sides into the ends of the plyboard and made a little fence across the middle of the trailer. The pieces over lapped in the middle so he nailed them together. "We gotta keep them balanced on each sida this axel," he sez. "That's another idea I got from that jug a-shine. You jest don't get good shine like that very often." We run the other six up on the trailer and Press-tone closed the tailgate. We wuz ready to go.

Press-tone eased down the gravel lane to the main road. I kept a-lookin' back at the trailer and ever thing seemed okay. Hit rode even better on the blacktop. I tol' Press-tone that ever thang looked good. "A-course they do," he sez. "That jug a-shine has done got me to think all this out. We only got 'bout three mile to the stock barn. We'll jest go straight through Milton. They's only one stop light and the barn's only 'bout a half mile tother side of it.

Things wuz goin' so good that I quit a-lookin' back at the trailer. As we wuz a-gettin' into Milton, we seemed to be a-slowin' down but the engine seemed to be a-runnin' faster. "How fast does you think we's a-goin'?" sez Press-tone.

"Well, a-judgin' by the fence posts and mail boxes a-goin' by, I'd say 'bout 35 or so," I sez.

"Then somethin' ain't right," he sez. "My speed-o-meter says 85."

I turnt 'round and looked at the trailer and I sez. "Lordy mercy, Press-tone, them hogs has done knocked down yore middle fence and they's all in the back and got that front end hiked up so high 'til yore back wheels ain't even on the ground." Well, Press-tone hit the brakes which he shouldn't orta done. They caught jest enough ta make all them hogs come ta the front and drop it down. I's a-tellin' you them rear tars musta been a-goin' 'bout 80 when they hit that ass-fault. I ain't never heard such schreechin' in all my life. And the smoke rose up like a brush far and the smell was somethin' fierce. The truck took off like one a them drag racers I seen one Sunday afternoon at the track over at

Calhoun. My head snapped back and I guess woulda gone out the back winder iffen it hadn't a-hit Press-tone's shotgun in the gun rack. The gun went off and blowed a big hole in the side of the cab on the driver's side.

Well, hit didn't take long fer that ass-fault ta run through what little tread wuz on them tars and git down to the rims. They give better traction but they didn't stay on the ground too long cause that sudden jump forward throwed the hogs to the back liftin' the wheels up again. Thas when all sorts of bolts and gear pieces begun to fly outa the truck's rear end. 'Bout that time Press-tone lost control and we run out through the bar-ditch and up against a culvert. The trailer jackknifed and tipped over a-spillin' all them hogs out into one big pile.

Press-tone jumped out a-yellin' some words that ain't fit for the ears of women-folk and chillun. The hogs seemed sorta addled from all the jerkin' about and we had 'em sorta piled up 'tween the truck and the trailer and the culvert. I thought we shoulda kept them thar as best we could 'til we could git some hep but Press-tone warn't a-havin' none a that. As I has done said many-a-time, "that man couldn't organize a piss-off in a brewery." So, he grabbed up a dead tree limb from outa the ditch and sez, "Taint fer to the stock barn. We kin jest drive 'em on down the road." Afore I could stop him he started in to pesterin' them hogs with that limb and got 'em all stirred up and a-runnin' up the road. A course hit wasn't nothin' fer me to do but ta grab up a nother limb and try ta hep 'im.

Anyways, the hogs were a-stayin' in the road pretty good 'til cars come along a-blowin' they horns and the drivers a-hollerin' at us and the hogs. This set them to a-runnin' off in all directions and things started to be like a-tryin' to herd a flock of cats. I tried to head those back up on the rat side of the road but I learnt pretty quick that when a 500 pound hog sets his mind to go someplace, a dead tree limb ain't too much of a hindrance. One of 'em took a notion to go through Miz Perkins' yard where she was a-hangin' out clothes on the line. He got hung up in a sheet and some other stuff and ended up a-pullin' the whole line down and a-draggin' hit and all the clean clothes two yards over afore he got loose from it. Miz Perkins wuz a-jumpin' up and down and a-screamin' and a-throwin' clothes pins at me and the hog but I didn't have the time rat then to stop and console her none.

Hit seemed like all the commotion set some of the hogs a-lookin' fer a refuge to git into and hide. Thas what happened at the boo-teaks. Thas what that new woman in town calls that little store she'd jest opened which was full of all them frilly clothes fer women. Anyways, she opened the screen door and looked out to see what wuz a-causin ' all the fuss and the first thang she saw wuz a big Poland-China a-headin' rat fer her shop. She started a-screamin' and slammed the door but that screen warn't no impediment to that hog. He went in and made about three rounds inside afore he come out with some of them lacy thangs a-hangin' onto 'im. He still had 'em on when they caught 'im down by the stock barn.

But the worst thang that happened on my side of the road wuz at the funeral home. They wuz jest a-finishin' up old man Sol Hankins funeral and they had them double wide doors open and wuz a-carryin' the casket out to put it into the hearse. Two big Hampshires run in them doors and mowed down them pall bearers like they wuz pins in a bowlin' alley. When the casket hit the ground, the lid popped open and old Sol come out like he'd been raptured. All the screamin' soon turned the two hogs on up the road.

By this time half the men in town wuz out with ropes, brooms, rakes, sticks, and all manner of stuff either a-drivin' or a-catchin' hogs. When the main herd went through the intersection, the light wuz red but the hogs didn't pay it no mind. Everbody finally got 'em drove up to the fence at the stock barn and then put 'em into some empty pens. There wuz only 11 of 'em. A couple of fellows said they saw two of 'em a-headin' down into Slab Town and they said they warn't about to go down thar and mess with them folks. The section got it's name from the folk a-usin' log slabs from the saw mill as sidin' fer they houses. I think they have quit a-doin' that but they's still a rough bunch of people. Anyways, somebody said they'd have those hogs butchered and the meat divided up amongst themselves afore dark.

The Sheriff come and 'rested both me and Press-tone. We wuz charged with a whole page of things. I tole him that them warn't nonna my hogs, that I wuz jest a-helpin' Press-tone. He said that made me some sort of a cessory, whatever in the hell that is. I didn't know that wuz any kind of crime but hit must be 'cause he put me in jail. He put us in different cells which wuz good 'cause I wuz a-thinkin' seriously 'bout a-killin' ol' Press-tone. But I have calmed down a rat smart now and see that that would only put him out of his misery.

Folks been a-comin' by the jail all afternoon a-givin' the Sheriff lists of things that the hogs ruint or tore up. Some of 'em talked about suin' for pain and sufferin', whatever that is. I suppose hit may a-been somethin' like when Miz

Hankins peed in the floor at the funeral home. Some even talked about a lynchin' but the Sheriff put that down pretty quick.

I think ol' Press-tone's gonna come out way behind on this escapade. He's in jail and the hogs is in the stock barn. They couldn't sell 'em on Tuesday 'cause they didn't have no papers on 'em. So, Press-tone's gonna hafta pay a whole week of boardin' fees until next week's sale. And with two of 'em gone to Slab Town, I's sure he won't git enough to pay the boardin' and auction fees, plus put a new rear end and wheels on his truck, plus payin' fer all the things the hogs tore up. Yessir, I'm a-tellin ' you, if hit don't involve one of those night waitresses from out at the truck stop or a jug a-shine, you'd best stay clear of ol' Press-tone Murphy or you're jest likely to become a cessory and to find yore sorry ass a-settin'in jail.

02
THE WHUPPIN'

Rebecca Bingham sat at her desk and cried quietly. She wanted to break down and sob loud enough to be heard over in Hancock County, but she restrained herself. She didn't know why. There was no one around to hear her. The children had been gone for over half an hour and the little schoolhouse and small clearing in which it sat were deserted. The only break in the silence was the chirping of birds and two squirrels barking at each other. The quiet crying did give her a feeling of control over something—and she needed that since she seemed to have lost control of everything else.

She leaned back in her chair, dabbed at her eyes with the damp handkerchief, and looked around the rather spartan room. It was typical of the many one-room schoolhouses that dotted the rural landscape of Tennessee: one room with adjoining cloakroom, wood stove in the center, grades 1 through 8, 37 students, one teacher.

This was her first appointment and she just had to succeed. These children needed to learn something more than what was over in the next hollow. The boys coming home from The Great War bringing stories about cities like New York and Paris and all the sights they'd seen told Rebecca that there was a whole other world outside of Hawkins County. And she wanted to be the one to awaken these youngsters to it. But, so many of them—especially the older ones—did not want to wake up. By the time they reached their mid-teens, most were as resistant to change and as suspicious of anything different as their elders were. Zack Bloodworth was one of these.

Zach was short for Zacharias. Rebecca suspected that the King James Bible was the source of all the names of the Bloodworth children. His sister, Hannah, was in the fifth grade. Zach was sixteen and in the fourth grade—not because he was dumb but because of his sporadic attendance pattern.

He had challenged her authority from the very first day and seemed determined to allow the school to operate only on his terms. Since he was older and physically stronger than most of the other boys, they tended to follow him. Rebecca had tried everything she knew to try and nothing had worked. Each attempt to subdue him or win him over had left him more defiant. Earlier that afternoon the time that she had been dreading for weeks finally came. She could take no more and stood face to face with him in the middle of the room and shouted in anger, "Young man, you will stay after school and get the whipping you deserve."

As soon as she said it, she wished she could take it back but it was too late for that. Since all the students had heard her, there could be no turning back. She also knew that she'd be flying in the face of local custom. By age sixteen, boys were considered to be men and no longer to be punished by females. Zach would probably accept blows from a stick or strap wielded by a man but a paddling from a woman might be more than he was willing to endure.

As the time for dismissal drew near, Rebecca wondered if he'd stay behind. He might just leave and never return to school. In many ways she hoped he would. But when she dismissed classes, Zach sat alone at his desk. She busied herself marking some spelling papers until the other children were out of earshot. Then she called him up to her desk.

"Zach, I'm sorry it's come to this but you have left me no choice." Her voice was shaking.

"Miz Bingham, you'uns know hit ain't right fer you'uns tah whup me. But I's a'gonner letcha 'cause you'uns are the teacher." With that he took his tin of Prince Albert tobacco out of his left rear pocket and bent over her desk.

Rebecca got shakily to her feet and picked up the three-foot hickory paddle. She swung it with as much force as her 95-pound frame could muster. She gave him four licks. The blows must have hurt him because he flinched noticeably on the last three.

When it was finished, Zach stood up and re-pocketed the Prince Albert. His face showed a mixture of hurt and anger as he said, "My daddy'll take care of you'uns," before stomping out the door.

Rebecca dried her eyes for the last time and prepared to leave. She dreaded what tomorrow might bring—maybe the end of her short teaching career, maybe the end of her. One seemed no worse than the other.

Zach came to school the next day. His behavior was noticeably better but he had an odd look in his eyes. They seemed to be saying, "Jest you'uns wait. This thang ain't over yet." And Rebecca feared that it wasn't.

The recitation went well that morning causing her to push her concerns about Zach into the background. Then, about mid-morning she noticed two or three students furtively punching their neighbors and pointing toward the road. She pretended not to notice but as she moved among the students, she turned so that she could glance in that direction. Her heart jumped up in her throat. Three rough looking men were walking up the road. Rebecca prayed that they would go on by but they turned into the buggy path that led up to the schoolhouse.

She continued the lessons as if she had not seen the visitors, but her heart began to pound and she could hear the blood rushing past her ears. Its sound was not unlike the nearby creek flowing over the large boulders after a heavy rain.

The men stopped outside the door and wiped their feet. As they entered, they removed their wide-brimmed straw hats, nodded politely to Rebecca, filed to the rear of the room, and seated themselves on a vacant bench. One was older. Rebecca guessed about 45 or 50. The other two looked to be somewhere in their 20s. Probably Zach's father and two of his older brothers. She glanced at Zach. The earlier odd look had turned into a smirk.

Since geography was usually Zach's best subject, Rebecca called him forward to recite his geography lesson for the day. She was thankful that his recitation was better than normal.

After sending him back to his seat, she called for the morning recess. The rest of the children hurried out to the playground but Zach remained in his seat.

"Zach, wouldn't you like to go outside?" Rebecca asked.

Before he could answer, the older man said, as the trio

got to their feet, "We-uns 'ud like fer him to stay, ma'am." With that they marched to the front of the room and lined up in front of Rebecca's desk, the older man in the middle. They all held their hats in front of their bodies with both hands on the brims. The last thing Rebecca wanted was for Zach to be a witness to the impending confrontation, but she felt powerless to alter the situation. Some of the more curious children were running back and forth to the schoolhouse and peeking in the windows or around the door facing.

She got to her feet, drew herself up to her full five feet two inches, and resolved to face whatever was coming as bravely as she could. Zach was visible between two of the men. The smirk was still on his face.

The older man began to speak. "Miz Bingham, I's Jacob Bloodworth an' these here's mah sons, Jonah and Micah." (Rebecca noted that she had been correct about the naming practices of the Bloodworth family.) "Zach tells me that you'uns whupped 'im yestiddy. Kin you'uns tell me whut fer?"

Rebecca tried to speak without her voice trembling. "Yes, Mr. Bloodworth, I can. Yesterday morning I caught him throwing spitwads three times while other classes were reciting. He also dipped one of Jessie Wainwright's pigtails into his inkwell. And in the afternoon he tripped Sam Jessup as he was coming to the front to recite. Sam fell into the stove and knocked the pipe loose and got soot all over everything. I'm sorry I had to paddle him, but I just couldn't take any more of this misbehavior."

Mr. Bloodworth looked at Rebecca for several seconds before turning his head toward Zach. "Is 'at right, boy?"

"Yessir," came the reply.

He turned back toward Rebecca. "Well, now, Miz Bingham, you'uns know Zach's sixteen year old. Hit ain't right fer you'uns to whup 'im. So, thar jest ain't no need fer you'uns tah giv'em no more whuppin'. You'uns know whut I'm a sayin'?

"Yes, yes, I think I do Mr. Bloodworth." Rebecca knew that her teaching career was over. Without the authority to deal with her main problem, her days at the school were numbered.

"'At's gud. Iffen Zach cuts up anymore, you'uns jest send word home by Hannah an' me an' his brothers'll whup the livin' daylights out of 'im. We-uns won't have 'im givin' ya no more trouble. Thank you'uns kindly fer ya time, ma'am." With that, the three turned as one, marched out the door, and headed up the buggy path toward the road.

Rebecca was both shocked and speechless. Her knees felt like jelly on a warm plate in July. She almost fell into her chair.

She looked at Zach. The smirk was gone. His chin had dropped to his chest and there was a look of utter disbelief on his face. She tried to keep her voice as even as she could. "Zach, don't you think you'd better go outside before you miss most of recess?" He got up and slunk out the door looking like a whipped puppy with its tail between its legs.

Rebecca leaned back in her chair as the feelings of relief and several other emotions flooded over her. The sounds of children at play drifted in from the playground. Perhaps she did have a future in teaching after all.

03
THE OLIPHANTS

They came to the ridge in '33. Some say it was '32. There used to be some argument over the year—not that it makes much difference. Truth of the matter is, in the depths of the Depression, folks were occupied full-time trying to scratch out a meager living. Few cared exactly what year they came. One day they just seemed to be there—hunkered down on each side of the ridge road, putting their imprint on the land. Petey Hawkins, who had had one year of college before the '29 crash wiped out most of his family's assets, said that they had come upon the scene like the Goddess Athena—full blown and fully armed out of the forehead of Zeus. Nobody knew what he was talking about, so they just made fun of him. But old Miz Junie May Buckhalter said to leave him be. That it was nice to see a person get some good out of higher education. Anytime one of the Oliphants was asked where they'd come from, he would just sweep his arm toward a distant horizon—the direction didn't seem to matter—and reply, "The mountains." So, folks just quit asking and started making up their own stories.

No one knows how they found the ridge. They just showed up one day at the County Clerk's office and wanted to buy the place for back taxes. Since they had cash money, the Clerk could hardly refuse. Some said it was illegal money. Had to be. Maybe stolen or made selling whiskey or some other illegal product. Their ragged clothing and two old trucks piled high with house plunder and dirty children argued against possessing any amount of legal cash. There wasn't much money in the county. Both banks were closed and the stove plant and sawmill were paying off in script. Maybe the Oliphants had robbed a bank someplace before it closed. Yep, it had to be illegal money.

Fortunately there was a good spring on the place. Still is in fact and still used by the Oliphants to this very day. They set up temporary quarters near the spring under some ragged canvas they'd made into tents. Once established, they began to scour the countryside for old lumber, rusty tin from barns, and any other materials which could be used in building. When they thought the pile large enough, they began their houses.

The first was for Hubert. He and his wife, Bessie, had several children of various ages and sizes. No one seemed to know exactly how many. Folks said Hubert and Bessie didn't even know. Their numbers seemed to vary with the seasons. Their house had four rooms and a front porch.

Across the road and about a hundred yards to the East, they built a two-room structure for Diamondback Oliphant and his wife, Sadie. They had no offspring. Never did have any. Some folks said it was because they smelled so bad they couldn't stand to get that close to each other. Others said that was not the reason since they both smelled equally bad and that body odor didn't seem to slow Hubert and Bessie down any. But many thought it was just nature's way of not overpopulating one county with too many Oliphants. Anyway, Diamondback's house was built up high on blocks. The underneath part served as shelter for pigs and chickens. And because they ran out of lumber, it had no front porch. Diamondback just leaned some scrap boards up below the door and used them to scramble up and down.

No one ever knew Diamondback's real name or even if he had one. It was said he was called that because he went to a church where snakes were handled. Said he could take up the rattler with the best of 'em. Said he would even let it crawl around in his shirt. "Course, no one ever saw him do it—or even go to church. But that's what folks said.

The Oliphants cultivated what little bottomland there was on the place plus the hillsides that were not too steep and had enough soil to plow. They raised mostly tobacco and corn. Folks said they had to be turning the corn into moonshine. They prodded the sheriff to catch them doing it, thinking this might be a way to rid the county of Oliphants once and for all. And the sheriff tried. He really did. But he never could locate a still on the Oliphant place. They never sold any 'shine locally either. Folks said they were making it and then hauling it to a distant county to sell. Petey Hawkins said that didn't make any sense because there was more local demand than there was supply. "Course nobody paid any attention to Petey. Said he was just a good example of too much learning addling his brain. So they just kept on trying to figure out exactly where the Oliphants were hauling their phantom cargo—and making up more stories about the Oliphants in the process. After all, it was the Depression and folks had to find something to amuse themselves with.

What little farm equipment the Oliphants had was old, worn out cast-offs. They got it mostly from farmers who were up grading. As a result, their equipment was usually about thirty years behind everyone else's. They would work on it enough to make it operate for a few years and then, when it was totally beyond working, they would "put it out to pasture." The "pasture" was the seven or eight acres surrounding their houses which they used for hay and pastureland. The dead piece of equipment would just be dragged out someplace in the pasture and left to the elements. Weeds and small trees soon would grow up through and around it. Their worn out farm trucks found the same grave sites. After a few years the Oliphants' pasture became an outdoor museum of early twentieth century farm equipment.

And that was not all. Collected building supplies such an concrete blocks, bricks, lumber, and tin were stacked randomly about the pasture as well awaiting any construction project that might strike the Oliphants' fancy. The areas close to their houses also served as repositories for all manner of cast-off things. There were stacks and piles of just about anything a person could imagine. This collection of junk soon became an Oliphant trademark. When asked one day why they had so much "stuff" on their place, Hubert replied, "Well, we believe in never throwin' nothin' away. You jest never kin tell when you might need it—or maybe a piece of it."

Folks soon found out that the Oliphants were honest in a perverse sort of way. That is to say, if they were around another farm or in a store in town, they wouldn't think of making off with anything that did not belong to them. However, there were certain situations in which they seemed to follow a different set of laws. One of these had to do with livestock.

They raised chickens, pigs, and goats which they kept around or under their houses. These were not a problem—but the mules and cows were. The Oliphants had two pair of mules and several head of cattle. It was common for farmers to let these animals forage in the cornfields in the fall and winter after the crop had been gathered. Nothing wrong with this—except the Oliphants generally let theirs forage in their neighbor's cornfields—and for some reason could see nothing wrong in doing so.

When they came to the ridge, not much of the land in the area was fenced. This suited the Oliphants just fine. They couldn't be blamed if their livestock turned up in somebody's cornfield which happened quite often. Folks began to suspect that the Oliphants' animals had some human direction in locating the best foraging fields. So, their neighbors began to fence their lands that joined the Oliphants. You would think this would keep the Oliphants' livestock at home but such was not the case.

In the late fall, a sturdy wire fence which had stood strong and tall for quite sometime would suddenly succumb to a falling limb. Oliphant livestock were always quick to find the breach and in a "good" year might forage for a month or more before they were discovered. The Oliphants were always glad to come and drive their animals back home and even to help repair the fence. After all was back in order, it was not unusual for another limb to fall on another neighbor's fence and the process repeated. It didn't take long for the Oliphants' neighbors to figure out that their fences were being cut, a limb thrown in the break, and the livestock driven through. It was frustrating—knowing what was going on and not being able either to prove it or to stop it. But the Oliphants reckoned not with Charlie Lattimore.

It seemed to Charlie that he had a broken fence most every year and he was tired of it. He determined to bring the

Oliphants to justice not only for his own peace of mind but also for the benefit of the whole community. His quest was a noble one. So, he formulated a plan.

That fall, as soon as he'd pulled all his corn, he began his fence patrol. He engaged Jim Teasdale, a neighbor who had no common fence line with the Oliphants, to assist him. He'd need a witness who had no bone to pick with the Oliphants. Every afternoon the two men would walk Charlie's fence line and document their trek. They'd only been patrolling about two weeks when late one afternoon, they came upon the scene of the latest Oliphant crime—a large beech limb across the broken fence. It was obvious that the wires had been cut. Charlie wound some tape around the wires near the cuts and took his wire cutters and clipped off about a foot of each wire of evidence. You could tell he'd read a lot of detective stories.

Then, he just walked around looking at the scene for a few minutes. "You notice anything strange?" he asked Jim.

"Naw, I don't guess I do."

"Well, this here's a beech limb, ain't it?"

"Sure is."

"You see any beech tree close by?"

"No, now that you mention it, I don't"

"I don't either. The nearest one I see is that big 'un 'bout fifty yards up the hill there. We'll need to pace if off to be exact. And look at that trail through the leaves where they dragged that limb down here to the fence."

Jim verified all that Charlie observed and Charlie wrote it

down. Jim could tell that he was enjoying playing detective. "Yes sir, I think we've got 'em," Charlie observed. "In the morning as soon as I get these Oliphant animals out of my cornfield and this fence back up, I'm going to town to see the judge."

Charlie was true to his word. His claims of property damage and loss went to Small Claims Court. His case came up at the end of the month.

Now, in this court there was no jury or attorneys. Each party just presented his case to the judge who made a ruling. Charlie did present a good case. He went through all his evidence and had Jim to verify everything. The only fly in the ointment was one of his old mules who had found the break in the fence and strayed up to the Oliphant place. Charlie had no idea why a mule would leave a perfectly good cornfield to wander amongst the piles of Oliphant junk, but he did. Charlie thought it would be good idea to own up to his fact during his presentation, which he did.

It was now Hubert Oliphant's turn. He did have on a pair of clean overalls but his old flannel shirt had so many patches that it was hard to discern its original pattern. His muddy work shoes looked as if they'd just come from the barn lot—and they smelled like it, too. The removal of his hat revealed a shock of dirty, matter hair and it was obvious his face had not had the benefit of a razor for several days.

He began, "Mister Judge, I's sorry to be here takin' up yore time today. I's jest a pore man a' tryin' to scratch out a livin' up on Sycamore Ridge. I knows these gud people's fences has done been broke down a lot, but ever time I comes an' gits my stock an' heps 'em put they fences back up, my stock is jest so pore an' hungry that they jest natchurly find them holes an' go down where the foragin' is good. Lordy knows, I wouldn't break down no man's fence that he'd done worked hard puttin' up. Times is jest so hard an' we is jest tryin' to do rat." Hubert's voice had begun to quiver with emotion and tears began to run down into the stubble on his cheeks. He took out a red bandanna and began wiping his face and blowing his nose. As he continued, there were audible sobs between some words as he continued to sponge his face.

An' Mister Judge, this las' time wuz real bad. The worse thang wuz that mornin' when I woke up an' looked out in the yard an' seen Mista Lattimore's ole mule jest a' standin' there a' peeing on Grandpaw's grave." Hubert broke down at this point, buried his face in the bandanna, and could not continue.

Charlie was amazed. He knew it was all a pack of lies. No one had ever seen an older person around the Oliphant place. And everyone knew what the Oliphants had been doing for several years. But, in spite of what he knew, Charlie felt sorry for Hubert Oliphant and his rag-tag clan. Then, he got mad at himself for feeling sorry for them. But, how he felt really didn't matter. The Judge threw the case out of court.

Even being hauled into court didn't slow the Oliphants down any. Fences continued to go down on a regular basis during foraging season. And when it happened to him, Charlie Lattimore went and got the Oliphants who drove their livestock back on to their land and helped Charlie fix the fence. Charlie didn't even get mad anymore. He just told his wife he figured that was just his contribution to a local charity.

A couple of years after the court incident, Jenny Lattimore approached her husband about doing something for the Oliphant children at Christmas. "No matter what people think of the Oliphants, the children have needs," she stated. Charlie agreed, so Jenny began her mission project. She got the names, ages, and approximate sizes of Hubert and Bessie's children. Then, she enlisted the aid of several other families in the community. They made up packages of clothing, toys, and candy for each child and took them over to the ridge a week or so before Christmas. Of course, the visit and gifts caused considerable excitement among the Oliphant children. Bessie seemed very appreciative. Hubert was not about—on purpose some of the women said.

During the visit one of the women noticed one of the little girls who had unsightly black patches around her mouth. The lady remarked to Bessie, "That sure is a pretty little girl. It's too bad she has that birthmark around her mouth."

"Oh, that ain't no birthmark," responded Bessie. "She jest et too many berries whiles we uz pickin' blackberries las' summer."

Apparently, cleanliness was not particularly high on the Oliphants' list of things to do.

Along about the time of the Christmas mission, Hubert came into conflict with the county hospital. Bessie got so sick that she had to go to a doctor. This was unusual because the Oliphants only went to doctors as a <u>last</u> resort. Folks said that one time Hubert even set Diamondback's broken arm. And it was not uncommon to observe the children sporting all manner of home-applied bandages and slings. Anyway, Bessie had to be bad off—and she was because the doctor put her in the hospital for about a week so he could get her cured.

Now, this didn't sit well with Hubert. He couldn't see why Bessie had to go to a hospital where they charged you money just to lay around in a bed when you could do that at home. And anyway, he had not taken her to the hospital—only to the doctor. This line of reasoning led him to feel responsible for the doctor's fee but not those of the hospital. So, he paid the doctor but when it came time for Bessie to go home, he slipped her out of the back door and ignored the bills the hospital sent each month for a year. The hospital administrator finally admitted defeat and quit sending the bills but he resolved never to get caught off guard again by any of the Oliphants. His vigilance was soon to pay off.

In a year or so, Bessie was getting ready to have another baby. Hubert went for the doctor who came out to their place to make the delivery. Things did not go well and there were a number of complications. The doctor had no choice but to take Bessie to the hospital for the delivery. Again, Hubert wasn't happy about the situation.

Resolving not to be stung again, the administrator ordered the baby to be kept in the nursery, to be only taken to Bessie for nursing, and never to be left alone with any of the Oliphants. They even took all of Bessie's street clothes away. Sure enough, when it came time for Bessie to leave, Hubert slipped up to her room and said, "Here, I brung 'ya some clothes. Put these on an' we'll git out the back before they see us."

"But, we can't leave without the baby. They got him in the nursery," Bessie responded.

"Aw, jest come on, begged Hubert, "jest leave 'im. I'll hep ya' make uh 'nother one when we git home."

Bessie may have been an Oliphant but she would not leave her baby behind. Reluctantly, Hubert went down to the checkout office and paid the bill—but not before he accused the administrator of holding his baby for ransom.

As the years passed, not much changed up on Sycamore Ridge but the county began to change around it. The years of prosperity after World War II brought more money and people into the area. In the sixties and seventies the county embarked on a program to widen and pave all its rock roads. Landowners were glad to give land for the widening so that they could have better roads. That is, all landowners except the Oliphants.

The rock road that ran up on Sycamore Ridge and through the Oliphant property was crooked and narrow and one of the worst in the county. But the Oliphants refused to give the county any land on either side for road improvement. It was not that the land was any good—it was mostly rock—or that they were using it for anything. It was the principle of the thing—Oliphants did not believe in giving anything away. So, the county improved the road up to the Oliphant property on both ends leaving the road and the Oliphants as a reservoir of backwardness surrounded by a sea of progressiveness. And so they remained.

As the twentieth century drew to a close more people from the city began to come into the county. They had money. They bought large sections of land, cleared the underbrush, and put up board fences. Soon there were black, red, white, and green fences surrounding much of the property in that section of the county. But the Oliphant place remained, looking about like it had looked in the thirties, sticking out like a sore thumb on the manicured hand of the nineties.

One day a black fence was built along one end of the Sycamore Ridge road. Then, a few months later another black fence appeared along the road on the other side of the ridge. Mr. Gaylord Timmons, an investment banker from the city, was putting his mark on the land. And the Oliphant place was the unsightly blot that was keeping him from joining his holdings into one coherent whole. Of course, there was a way to take care of that. He'd always found that enough money would remove any obstacle. He'd simply buy the Oliphant place.

He did some asking around about this family and its history. He also tried to find out about their finances, but they didn't seem to have any accounts any place. With his research done, Timmons decided a direct approach would be best. He drove up to see Hubert Oliphant.

He parked his BMW just off the road and walked up the path to Hubert's house picking his way among the piles of cast-off debris, abandoned pick-up trucks, and rusting farm machinery. Some of the house's clapboards had fallen completely off, others were still attached at one end and hung down forming unusual geometric patterns. The front porch had disengaged itself from the house proper and pitched face first into the yard rendering the front door unusable. Its tin had been cannibalized and used to repair portions of the main roof. Hubert saw him coming and came out the back door and around the house to meet him. He offered Timmons a seat on a stack of scrap lumber. Timmons had never before conducted business in such a setting. He was glad he had not worn one of his best suits.

Timmons sensed that Hubert knew what he wanted, so he quickly cut to the chase and stated his business making Hubert a generous monetary offer. Hubert mulled it over for a few minutes while gazing out into the nearby woods. Finally he spoke. "Mista Timmons, you has done made a gud offer. You shore has. But, you know I's done lived on this place fer nigh on ta' sixty-five year. Me an' Bessie has done raised us a bunch of youngins' here. They's all done left now 'cept fer two. This is the onlyest real home we's knowed anythang about. Hit's jest lak hit's part of us."

Timmons interrupted, "I realize that this place has a lot of sentimental value for you and your loved ones. Because of that I'm willing to pay more." He made another offer much higher than his first.

Hubert had successfully parried Timmons' first thrust. How would be handle this one? His gaze returned to the woods and then moved to the yard in which they sat. His eyes began to water as he started to speak again. "You's' rat 'bout our feelin' 'fer this place, Mista Timmons. And I really 'preciates yore willingness ta' pay more. But, they's some other thangs, too." Tears were now running down his cheeks as he fetched his bandanna from his overall pocket and began to wipe his face. The scene was reminiscent of the courtroom drama of years past and of which Timmons knew nothing. "Ya' see, Mista Timmons, we is a' setttin' on holy ground. Ma' own grandpaw is buried rat here in this yard." Hubert was now crying openly.

Timmons looked around the yard. All he saw were weeds, trash, and piles of junk. There was no gravestone anywhere and no area that looked like a tended gravesite. "Where is he buried?" he asked.

Hubert was barely able to answer between the wiping and sobbing. "Thas the main problem, Mista Timmons, hit's done bin so long that we has done forgot."

Timmons made his way back to his car leaving Hubert sitting on the lumber and crying. He thought to himself, "Perhaps there's another approach that might work better."

The next day Timmons went to see the real estate agent who'd acted for him in the purchase of his other properties and related is experiences with Hubert Oliphant. "Hubert's not gonna sell," the agent stated flatly. "He'll just sit and cry and blubber and wipe his face and make up more lies."

"What about Diamondback," asked Timmons. "He's bound to have some ownership of the place and maybe he won't be as hard to deal with."

"I could talk with him. What sort of offer do you want me to make?"

"Tell you what we'll do," Timmons said. Start out with $2,000 an acre. Anybody around there would jump at the chance to sell rocky ridge land for that. But go on up to $10,000 an acre if you have to. It's highway robbery at that price but I want that land."

In a few days later, the agent went out to see Diamondback. It was obvious from the start that he was no more interested in selling than Hubert had been. But the agent gave it his best shot. The $2,000 offer was made which

Diamondback turned down. After time and some more talk, the agent inched the offer up a little, another refusal. Repeat the process. This went on for quite some time until, finally, the $10,000 offer was made along with the statement that that was as high as the agent was authorized to go. Diamondback leaned back against the tree he'd been sitting under and thought for a while before responding.

"I know hit's a gud offer—a real gud offer. Mor'n this place is worth most likely. An' I guess we'd take it iffen hit weren't fer two things." He paused as if to search his memory to find the two things he was speaking of. "One thang is we jest don't need the money." The agent couldn't believe his ears. How could they not need the money? Diamondback continued, "But that ain't the main thang. We jest lak this place. I 'spose we would sell iffen we thought we could find a' 'nother one we'd lak as well. But, you know, places lak this is hard to find these days." The agent knew Diamondback was right on this last point. He looked around at the piles of junk, rusting machinery, the dilapidated houses, and the scrawny animals. He just shook his head and headed back to town leaving Diamondback leaning against the tree.

As the twenty-first century opened, the Oliphants were still there hunkered down on both sides of the rock road on Sycamore Ridge—and the ridge much the same as it was in '33. It's unusual in this day and age to find people who are so content with their lot.

04
THE DECISION

Sadie Hazelwood pulled back the stringy curtains that covered the window over the kitchen sink and look out toward the barn. She didn't need a clock. The black and white cows ambling in from the pasture told her milking time was near. She set about getting the stuff together that this chore called for. There was little enthusiasm in her step. That emotion had been long replaced by a dogged determination. She just had to hold on for one more year.

Sadie was a widow woman. She'd been one going on two years now. She often wondered why Amos had gone and died and left her to face all these problems by herself. At first she was mad at him for doing it. But even in her anger she knew that such a feeling wasn't right. Then again, if he had just gone to the doctor with that indigestion and pain in his arm or taken better care of himself or if.... But he was just trying to save money and work toward the thing they both wanted more than anything else. She couldn't fault him for that—but she didn't bargain on losing him in the process.

They'd been together for forty-one years. Worked hard together in the fields. She looked down at her arms, brown and cracked like the sleeve of an old leather jacket. She knew that her face and neck looked the same. The sun had aged her past her sixty-three years. And now it was just her left to carry on—and she would carry on even if it killed her too.

Sadie picked up the pails and cloths and slipped on an old pair of tennis shoes as she opened the back door. The August afternoon was hot and she wore nothing but a light cotton housedress. But it didn't matter. There'd be nobody at the barn to see her. She also picked up the .22 rifle that stood in its regular place beside the door and put a handful of shells in pocket of her dress.

As she walked slowly toward the barn, her eyes surveyed all the 80-acre farm. It seemed so small, and it was much smaller than the 320 acres, a whole half section of land, that she and Amos had started out with—land that he hated to part with, but the parting had to be if they were to get the thing they wanted, and the thing they wanted was what Dolly wanted.

Dolly was their only child. She had come along late, long after they had given up hope. But they had not spoiled her. They taught her to work as they had been taught. By the time she was twelve, she could drive a tractor with the best of them and could put in a full day in the hot sun without complaining. Yes, Dolly was really something special.

But before she was very old, both Amos and Sadie knew that the farm would not be her life as it had been theirs. Dolly loved books and learning and showed a strong aptitude for both. Even before she got to high school, she had determined that she wanted to be a doctor. She began to volunteer at the hospital and especially liked working around the Emergency Room. Sadie thought she might be squeamish at the sight of all the blood but the early work with farm animals had prepared her for that. As best she could tell, human blood looked the same as animal blood.

However, Amos and Sadie knew that the main hindrance to Dolly's plans would be money rather than blood. They had some savings but the first year of college took most of that. Then, Amos turned to the only resource he had—his land. He began to sell if off in small parcels, forty or so acres at a time. It was good land and fetched a good price. Sadie knew how it hurt him to part with it and she once tried to console him about it. "Hit don't make no difference," was Amos' gruff reply. "We don't have nobody but Dolly to leave it to nohow. And she ain't gonna farm it. Best we use it to make her a doctor. Now, I don't want to hear nothing more about it." Sadie knew he was right. She also knew that he felt a sense of failure at not being able to hold the land and that he was determined to be successful with Dolly. They all worked to ensure that success.

Amos began to farm more intensely, to raise more beans and corn and hay for sale rather than just to feed the dairy herd. He put off buying new equipment and making major repairs on the buildings. He wore his clothes until they were threadbare and refused to see a doctor until it was too late. And Sadie toiled beside him doing a man's share of the work.

Dolly did her part as well. Her grades earned some scholarship monies each year. She also got a job to pay for her clothes and living expenses. But as she got further into med school, the academic pressure increased and her contributions grew smaller and the land began to go faster.

Sadie got to the barn and paused for a moment letting her eyes survey the last eighty acres—the last and probably the best piece of the whole farm. It was to be used when Dolly finished her residency and started her practice and Sadie was determined to hold on until then.

Most of the land had been bought by Hugo Gerthman, a

man who had migrated to their community a few years earlier and started raising beef cattle. He was a good farmer but somewhat arrogant and overbearing. Amos said that he was glad that his land would be in the hands of a good farmer, but he had no real liking for Gerthman. Of late he had seemed impatient—too impatient—to get his hands on the last eighty acres.

Sadie opened the sliding door and let the first two cows into the milking area. She washed their udders and hooked them up to the old milking machine. She cocked her head and listened to the sound of the milker. An untrained ear would have detected nothing amiss but Sadie's picked up the slightly irregular, grating sound that told her the machine was laboring toward another failure. She hoped it wouldn't play out on her today and leave her to finish the job by hand.

Her concern about the milking machine caused her to think of Kwapinsky. She didn't like even to think about him. From the first she'd never liked him, never liked anything about him right down to his name. What kind of name was Kwapinsky anyway? It wasn't even American. How did a man with a name like that get to Tennessee?

As her dislike for him grew, Sadie supposed that she actually hated him. She wasn't sure if what she felt was really hate. In all her days, Sadie had never hated anyone as far as she knew. But she also knew she had never felt as she did about anyone else. If the burning in her gut was hate, he'd earned it.

Kwapinsky was charged with inspecting dairies for health and code violations and it seemed that he could always find something wrong around Sadie's barn. The time the milking machine broke down, he had come by just as she was finishing the last cow and had made her pour out all the afternoon's milk—even that which had been done by the machine. Sadie prayed that a breakdown and a Kwapinsky visit would never happen again.

One day it occurred to her that Kwapinsky was coming by more often than former inspectors had. She was about to decide that it was just her imagination when she overheard a disturbing conversation. She was in the back corner of Huff's Country Store looking for some buttons for a dress she was making. Several local loafers were sitting around the pot-bellied stove swapping stories. Sadie was hidden from their view and was paying little attention to them until she heard Kwapinsky's name mentioned. She listened as one of the farmers related what Kwapinsky had said one night when he'd had a few too many beers at a nearby roadhouse. Said Gerthman had put him on his payroll and all he had to do was just give some "special attention" to Sadie's dairy.

Now it all made sense—Gerthman's growing impatience and the frequent inspections. Gerthman wanted the last eighty acres and he wanted it quickly. If the dairy went under, Sadie would have no choice but to sell and sell at Gerthman's price. It was that day that she first felt the burning in her stomach. And the burning had grown more intense with every Kwapinsky visit and more intense with every check she had to pay for the corrections of the violations he found. Yes, it had to be hate.

Sadie had lain awake many nights trying to figure out a solution. But none would come to her mind. She was just an old widow woman with a ramshackle dairy and no proof.

They might beat her but they'd never make her quit. Amos would be proud of her for that.

As the machine worked on the second pair of cows, it began to sound better. Sadie felt a sense of relief but the burning did not diminish. She picked up the rifle, dropped a shell into the chamber, and moved around to the other side of the barn.

Amos had taught her to shoot. She had become almost as good a shot as he was. On many days she would accompany him to the barn and shoot rats while he saw to the milking. Her marksmanship had just about solved the rat problem but they had come back after Amos' death.

Sadie stood quietly for a few minutes in the dim light before she heard the scratching of a rat's claws on a rafter as he moved toward the area where the cow feed was stored. She knocked him off with one well-placed shot. A few minutes later another emerged from a hole near the outside wall. He only twitched a few times after the bullet passed through the center of his body. Sadie didn't like to waste ammunition and prided herself on seldom missing and even more on seldom having to shoot a rat more than once.

After putting two more cows on the machine, she returned to her hunting. She had been standing motionless for several minutes waiting for the next rat to show itself when her eye caught a movement outside through one of the cracks between the wallboards. She thought little about it thinking it was a bird until she saw it the second time. For some reason it didn't look right. Sadie walked over and put one eye up to one of the larger cracks.

Then she saw him. It was Kwapinsky. He liked to

surprise her at milking time but he usually drove up to the barn lot gate and Sadie could hear his truck when he started up the hill. This time he had parked over on the main road and was sneaking up from the back of the barn. If she hadn't been shooting rats, Sadie would never have known he was coming until he walked in on her. The burning in her gut got hotter.

Sadie moved over to the milking area to await him. He would come through the side door. She wanted to do something. But what? Kwapinsky was about as sorry an excuse for a person she'd ever known. She had no more respect for him that she did for the rats she'd just been shooting. She looked down at the sweaty housedress and the rifle she carried—and she knew what she would do. She hoped that Amos would forgive her.

Kwapinsky circled the barn trying to keep some cover between himself and it most of the time. That way he could drop down and hide in case Sadie came outside unexpectedly. The sound of the milking machine told him that she was inside. He covered the last few yards in a low crouch so that his shadow would not fall on the wall. He paused for an instant, took a deep breath, stood up, and jerked the door open. The old barn wall sagged downhill on the hinged side of the door and the force of Kwapinsky's pull plus gravity tore the handle from his hand causing the door to bang loudly against the side of the barn. He started to enter but what he saw inside made him freeze with one foot over the threshold.

The rays of the low afternoon sun streamed through the open door and threw a rectangular spotlight on the interior. Kwapinsky saw everything at once and all the parts separately at the same time. Sadie stood facing him with her left hand resting on the rump of one of the cows. On her feet were the dirty tennis shoes with their tongues sticking up at odd angles. But the part of the picture which seemed to draw his attention was the rifle in Sadie's right arm. The end of the barrel was a black hole that seemed to probe through his body. He expected to see flashes come from its depths and to feel its lead missiles tear into his heart and other vital organs.

For what seemed like an eternity, Kwapinsky could not move. He felt as if his feet were encased in concrete. But then, he knew that he had to move. As he whirled to escape, his foot found a fresh pile of cow manure which caused it to slide to one side, pitching him to the ground. He landed in another pile and rolled through a couple more before regaining his feet and his balance.

Kwapinsky ran harder than he had ever run in his life. He tried to vault the barn fence but was caught by the top strand of barbed wire. It tore one leg of his pants from hip to knee and sliced a long gash in the leg inside. He thought he heard several shots but if they hit him, he didn't feel anything.

He jumped into his truck without stopping to clean the cow manure off his clothes. He drove straight to Gerthman's house and barged in when his knock was not immediately answered. He didn't give Gerthman the opportunity to say anything—just told him to take him off the payroll, that he would not inspect Sadie Hazelwood's dairy again if she lived to be a hundred.

After delivering his message, Kwapinsky turned on his

heel and left, leaving Gerthman to stare at the fresh blobs of cow manure and spots of blood on his new Persian rug.

Sadie stood without moving, as the sounds of Kwapinsky's departure grew fainter. When she heard the roar of the truck engine and the squeal of the tires on the asphalt, she set the rifle down against a post and reached up and took her dress down off the nail where she'd hung it. After putting it on over her head, she picked up the rifle, dropped a shell into its empty chamber, and moved to the other side of the barn to see if any more rats were coming out of their holes. Yes, she hoped Amos would forgive her. Up to this day, he had been the only man she'd ever allowed to see her naked.

05
A RUDE AWAKENING

Miss Zadie Mae Tompkins is getting on up in years. Some of her organs and body parts have ceased to function at acceptable levels forcing her to reside in an assisted living facility but her mind has remained as sharp as ever. She likes to relate stories to anyone who will listen about her youth and the early years of her career. Herein lies the tale.

Miss Zadie Mae was born in the roaring 20s, came of age in the Great Depression of the 30s, and started her career in social work in the 40s. Her first job was in a rural county in East Tennessee. She was young and full of energy and it was well that she was. Most of her clients were welfare families who lived back up in the hills and hollows. Since they seldom came to town, it was up to the social worker to make the periodic reviews of each family by a personal visit. This was no easy task. There were no paved roads back into the hills; some had not even been rocked. Of course, there were no road signs or house numbers. However, each file generally contained directions to the client's house. It was not uncommon to read, "Don't visit after a heavy rain. The creek will be too deep to ford." Or "Take the left fork of the path. The other one leads to the family still."

So it was that one bright spring morning Miss Zadie Mae was assigned to review the file of Miss Hattie, an old lady who lived by herself back up in the hills. She had neglected to eat breakfast that morning but thought she'd be back in town by noon at the latest. Unfortunately, things did not quite work out that way.

To start with she got lost and like to have never found the old lady's cabin. And Miss Hattie was not much help in supplying the needed information. She was sure some of the dates were in the family Bible but could not seem to locate it even though she searched the cluttered cabin for almost an hour. Another time, Miss Hattie excused herself to visit the outhouse. When she failed to return after quite sometime, Miss Zadie Mae went looking for her. She found her in the garden weeding the onions. Miss Hattie had forgotten about her visitor and was busying herself with her chores.

As the time ran on into early afternoon, Miss Zadie Mae grew more and more frustrated—and hungry. Skipping breakfast had not been a good idea.

With the growling of her stomach growing louder and more frequent, Miss Zadie Mae's attention was drawn to a small bowl of shelled peanuts on the rickety table beside her chair. At first she just picked up one or two to nibble on. But as the time wore on she found her hand making more frequent trips to the bowl. By the time she was finished with Miss Hattie's file, she was embarrassed to note that she had also finished off the peanuts.

She felt so bad about eating poor old Miss Hattie's peanuts that she began to apologize. "Miss Hattie, I've just sat right here and eaten all your peanuts. I'm so sorry."

"Oh, don't you worry your head none about that, Dearie," replied Miss Hattie.

"But I <u>am</u> worried about it," responded Miss Zadie Mae, "I hope you'll forgive me."

"Why, hon, there ain't nothin' to forgive."

"Well, I feel so bad about it that the next time I come out here I'm gonna bring you some peanuts."

"Oh, honey, please don't do that. I can't eat 'em noway."

"You can't?"

"Naw. I ain't got no teeth. I jest like to suck the chocolate off of 'em."

06
THE PLANTATION

My early years, the late 1930s and early 40s, were spent on three plantations in the Mississippi Delta—that fertile, flat area of farmland which runs from Memphis southward to Vicksburg. The big River itself forms its western boundary. A range of low hills mark its eastern limits as it sweeps southeast, widening to fifty miles or so near Greenwood, before turning southwest to terminate at Vicksburg's bluffs. If the Delta, this ancient floodplain of the Mississippi, were the whole, the plantations were its most important parts.

First of all, it was a terrible breech of etiquette to call them "farms" and their owners "farmers" even if technically that's what they were. To the Delta landowners, those small land holdings in the Mississippi hill country were farms and the families who worked them were farmers. They themselves were "planters" who owned "plantations" of as much as one to two thousand acres and some even larger. These Delta planters and their families formed a social class unto themselves.

Seldom did a planter oversee his plantation. A manager would be employed to see to the day-to-day operations. That was my father's role although he did not hold that position when I was born. At that time he was a sharecropper.

Sharecroppers or croppers occupied the second lowest rung of the Delta's economic ladder. The colored farm tenants were relegated to the lowest. Most sharecroppers were only the latest of several cropper generations—poorly or non-educated, backward, producing large families, living close to physical and economic starvation, lacking either the skills or ambition to claw their way to a higher position. However, my father was not an ordinary sharecropper. He had had two years of college at Mississippi A and M which is today Mississippi State University. He quit college to manage one of the School's experimental farms and eventually wound up as a salesman and district manager for the Wrought Iron Range Company, maker of iron cook stoves and heaters. But the Depression took all this away, forcing him back to the land—land that would provide food but little profit in an era of depressed cotton prices.

I first saw the light of day on a damp, cold evening in December in a three-room shotgun house on Jabe Dunnaway's place near Anguilla. There were no hospitals. Doc Smith, a genuine country doctor, handled the delivery. He was my uncle as was Jabe.

By the mid 30s my father was sharecropping a large new ground farm back toward the River. As they opened new farmland, planters would often use sharecroppers until they were ready to incorporate it into their plantations. And "new ground" was an apt description of these areas. The land had recently been drained and cleared, had never known a plow, and was full of stumps and roots, making cultivation extremely difficult.

One of my early remembrances is helping to haul chunks of stumps to a large fire in the center of the cotton field.

The soil was not the sandy loam of the old Delta but buckshot, a rich, grainy soil which responded poorly to both wet and dry conditions. When wet, it clodded up, was slow to dry, and was extremely slick—"as slick as owl shit" I remember hearing one old fellow say. When dry, it would contract and break into spidery cracks an inch or so wide and several inches deep. But the black soil, only recently liberated from rank bayou waters, was rich and would produce a bumper crop of cotton in years when the weather was neither wet too late nor dry too early.

But late in the year 1937, that is after all the crops had been gathered, my world changed.

My father became the manager of Mr. E. J. Ganier's plantation located on Deer Creek at Percy, Mississippi. Percy was named for that Mississippi family which came to claim considerable political and literary fame after its founder, Charles Percy, hacked the original plantation out of the surrounding wilderness in the 1840s. Mr. Ganier was a smallish man of French descent who strutted about the place like a bantam rooster and whose facial features resembled one.

This plantation covered about two thousand acres, although some acreage was in woods and not under cultivation. My father managed three plantations at different times as I was growing up but they were all run the same. Later, when I studied history, I was struck by the similarities between the plantation and the medieval manor.

The rich, delta soil was worked by forty or so black families who lived in weather beaten tenant houses scattered over the landscape. Some were called "shotgun" houses because of the way the rooms were arranged—three or four rooms in a line one behind the other with a porch across the front. The last room was the kitchen; the others were combination sitting/sleeping rooms. There was no chimney but there were flues for a wood cook stove in the kitchen and for wood heaters in the other rooms. Water came from a pitcher pump in the back yard. The sanitary facility was a rickety outhouse somewhere out back. This was no frills living for sure but it was the going standard and so common that no one really thought about it.

Tenants with larger families usually were assigned square-shaped houses with a long porch across the front and maybe even a back porch. These would be four or five rooms with more space than a shotgun house afforded but, other than a chimney with a fireplace, everything else was about the same. Five or six sleeping in one room was not uncommon.

The manager's house was a step up from the large tenant house but not a huge step. There were some outbuildings: smoke house, chicken house, storage shed, and a garage, but no plumbing or electricity. We had a pump and an outhouse out back and used coal oil lamps for light. The Big House, the owner's residence, was the only building on the place with plumbing and electric lights. This was normal for the times.

Our house on the next plantation had plumbing and a Delco lighting system. Power was provided by a whole bunch of batteries located in one of the outbuildings. When the lights started to get dim, my father would start the gasoline engine that sat beside the battery building and charge the batteries. This would take several hours but only had to be done about once a week. With both plumbing and lights, we thought we were living in the lap of luxury. Our next place even had plumbing AND electricity. The Boyd family was moving to undreamed of heights

The land was cultivated by black labor using hoes and mule-drawn plows. There were two tractors which were used primarily to work the large block of the plantation reserved for the owners—the medieval demesne. Because of the plantation's dependence upon the labor of the black tenants, a good manager had to be able to attract and keep good workers. That's probably why my brother and I were instructed never to call one of the tenants "nigger" to his face. As Mama said, "Call them 'colored'; 'nigger' hurts their feelings." I cannot recall either of my parents ever calling a colored person "nigger" to his face, although the term was used freely around the house. I seldom used the word. For reasons I was yet to understand, I did not like the sound of it.

In December and January after the crops had been sold and farm work was minimal, my father began to "trade" with the tenants for the next crop year. On the designated days, they would gather in the back yard, come in the back door (never the front) one by one, and stand with hats in hand before my father who sat at the kitchen table with the account book. It was the day of economic reckoning. They were told what they had been "furnished" (advanced in money and goods against their crop) and what their crop (always cotton) had sold for. They were paid any profit in cash. A negative balance meant that they started the next year in the hole—if my father decided to "trade" with them for another year. If not or if they wanted to go to another plantation, the debt had to be paid by the other plantation before they could leave. The sheriff was sent after those who left with debts on the books. Also, there were few managers who would take a tenant without checking out his status with his previous manager. This union of the law and the dominant economic class kept the black laborers in a state of peonage. It was not legal or right but it was the way the system worked.

In the "trading" discussion, it was proper for the tenant to make certain requests, e.g., additional cotton acreage, more day work, etc., but it was strictly up to my father whether they were granted. He would write the terms in the ledger for his information but the agreement with the tenant was always verbal since it was rare to find one who could read or write. However, they could, with few exceptions, recite the terms of the "trade."

Some unscrupulous managers took advantage of this illiteracy and kept the books so that their tenants seldom got out of debt. Although uneducated, these folks were not stupid. They knew which managers tended to cheat their tenants and spread this knowledge by word of mouth throughout the colored community. As a result, these plantations found it difficult to get and to hold good tenants. During the "trading" times, there were always men from other plantations looking for a place with my father. "Yasser, Mista Luke, I's bin over on Mista Charlie Camp's plantation gwine on two years now. I jest needs mo' cotton land. I's got nine kids. Six kin do field work. An' Bessie Mae kin cook fer th big house. I's a good worker. Won't burn up yore house. Ya' ken as' Ike. I's bin knowin' him 'bout ten years."

And when word got around that my father would be leaving for another plantation, the back yard would fill with tenants asking, "Mista Luke, will ya' take me witcha when ya' go?"

In all the years of living on plantations, I can only remember one of my father's tenants "departing without leave." Sometime on Saturdays my father would take me with him. One October on such a Saturday, he took me and a group of eight or ten of our tenants to Jesse's house. It was a standard shotgun house with a chicken house and outhouse out back. Neither Jesse nor his wife was about. The men went through the house and hauled the meager furnishing out in the yard. Then my father divided them among the crew. The same division was made of the few scrawny chickens and the vegetables in the garden. As I was helping to pick the okra in the garden, I heard my father say, "We'll come back Monday and pick his cotton and pull his corn." This prompted me to ask the man who was working on the okra with me, "What happened to Jesse?" He rolled his eyes and looked all around before he spoke as if he were fearful of being overheard, "He's done runned off," he replied in a hushed, secretive tone. Nothing else was said. Nothing else needed to be said.

* * *

A plantation manager, with the backing of local authorities, had a great deal of power over his tenants. These colored folk had no power at all but they did possess one neutralizer—humor. They seemed to know instinctively that if they could keep the white man laughing he wouldn't be too hard on them. Many were good con men and would play the fool to keep their overseers amused. Although it did not happen on one of our plantations, the following incident is a good illustration of this tactic. Rufus was only in his late thirties but poor diet and no attention to oral hygiene had caused the loss of most of his teeth. In fact, he only had one upper front one left which hung there like a loose stalactite. When he grinned or laughed (which he did a lot), most of his gums were exposed and he had the habit of flicking the tooth from side to side with his tongue. One Saturday during pay time Rufus and some of the other men were joking with each other and Rufus was, of course, flicking his tooth. For some reason the manager was annoyed about something and became more so as he looked up from his ledger and money box and saw Rufus standing in front of him with a wide grin and the tooth in constant motion. "Damn you Rufus," he exclaimed, "I'm sick and tired of looking at that damned tooth!"

Rufus' grin disappeared. "Yasser, Boss."

"Here," the manager said as he counted out Rufus' pay for that week's day work, "I'm gonna give you an extra three dollars. I know you're going to town, so I want you to go by the dentist and get that thing pulled. I don't wanna see it come Monday morning. You understand me?"

"I sho' does Boss. Is gwine 'a do jes' lik you say. Yous done seen de las of hit. You sho nuff is." Rufus took the money and hurried away.

On Monday the manager was at the barn lot making work assignments when Rufus walked up. He still had his tooth. When the manager saw him, he was more than angry. "You sorry-assed field nigger! I gave you the money to get that damn thing pulled and you still got it. Why, I'm gonna . . .!" The other tenants began to gather around to see the showdown when Rufus interrupted, "I tried, Boss. I jes' done the bes' I could." He stood before his manager, his eyes downcast and his lanky frame in a humbled posture.

"Whatta you mean, you did the best you could?"

"Well, Boss, you know my woman Sadie is with child."

"Of course, I do, but what in hell has that got to do with anything?"

"Boss, I done went to dat tooff man. He look in my mouff an' he look me up an' down. He look me all over an' he say, 'Rufus, ain't you bin breedin?' an' I say 'I sho nuff is' an' he step back an' he say, 'I cain pull no tooff from a man whut's bin breedin". Hit jes' ain't right. You gonna hafta come back later afta you breedin' time is done.' An' dat's the Lord's Truff, Boss."

The manager knew the story was one big fabrication but he loved the way Rufus told it. He walked away chuckling. Rufus kept his tooth <u>and</u> the three dollars.

* * *

It was unusual for a colored tenant to own a car. Those who did generally had vehicles that looked as if they had been rescued from a junkyard or put together with parts from one. And they usually ran about the same way. They were always breaking down and two or three flat tires on a Saturday trip to town was not unusual. Most of the time an owner spent more time working on his vehicle than driving it. This is undoubtedly the source of the definition of "a colored weekend"—8 hours of f—king and 40 hours of fixing flats.

Charlie was the hostler who worked around the barns on one plantation and he had a car. It was a Model A Ford — one of those big square two-seaters with a spare tire mounted on the back. Most Saturdays I knew I could find

Charlie at his house close by the barn lot trying to get his car ready to drive to town. I liked to visit him on these days because he would let me help him. He taught me how to put patches on the inner tubes which were mostly patches to start with. Often Charlie's mechanical work on the engine was not of lasting quality. Sunday morning would find him knocking on our back door to get permission from my father to take one of the tractors or a team of mules to pull his car home.

If I ran out of inner tubes to patch on those Saturdays, I would go into Charlie's house and visit with Pearlie, his wife, who would usually be straightening her hair in preparation for the trip to town. She used two wood handled straightening irons and a kerosene lamp. While she used one, the other would be stuck down the lamp's chimney getting hot. She used some type of salve on her hair and when she pulled the hot iron through it, there was a lot of smoke and an usual smell. The process fascinated me. I expected to see her hair catch fire but, fortunately, it never happened.

One Sunday Charlie managed to drive his A Model all the way to the Memphis airport. Everyone was fascinated with aviation and Charlie and Pearlie had gone up to watch planes land and take off. There were not many commercial flights but it was the early 40s and there was plenty of military training going on at all airports. Charlie parked by the side of the road right at the end of a runway. He and Pearlie sat in the front seat watching the planes passing directly over them as they practiced take-offs and landings.

They had been there for a good while when they noticed a plane coming in very low. In fact, the plane looked as if it were about to fly through the car and before they could get out, it did. The plane's left landing gear hit the car in the left rear door and sheared away the rear of the car clear down to the frame. The plane made a safe landing. Charlie and Pearlie were left sitting in the front seat uninjured.

They had to get home by Greyhound bus the next day after selling the car to a junk yard for ten dollars. They were afraid no one would believe them but the story and picture in The Commercial Appeal verified their account of the event. Charlie had lost his car but he was the center of attention around the plantation for several weeks.

* * *

In late summer after the cotton was laid by, that is, after it required no further cultivation, it was time to cut the winter's supply of wood. Since everyone cooked and heated with wood, it was necessary to lay in a good supply before time for picking cotton and pulling corn and before the wet winter weather set in.

A section of the woods on the back of the place would be selected. Since my father also used this operation for clearing new farmland, everything was cut. The only tools used were crosscut saws and axes. The underbrush and limbs were piled and burned. The trees both large and small were hauled out by wagon and a share distributed to each tenant. There were two or three special wagons to haul the big trees; the small stuff was carried on the regular farm wagons. The decision as to how much wood each tenant got was my father's alone. If a tenant wanted more, he was free to use the mules and wagons and to cut more on his own time. The sawing of the large pieces into blocks to split for stove wood and fireplace sticks and the chopping up of the saplings was left to each tenant. They would share the labor on this, several working at each house until each one's pile was done.

Sometimes I got to go to the woods to watch the operation. I loved to see and hear the big trees fall and to marvel how the teams of mules could pull the large logs up the pole incline onto the heavy log wagons. Hardly a day passed that the crew didn't turn up a snake or two. Occasionally, there would be a rattlesnake and, if we were near a swamp, a cottonmouth, but most were harmless. Regardless, they all were killed. The vast majority of colored folk were deathly afraid of snakes and to them the only good snake was a dead snake.

The tenants were not paid for their labor in wood cutting. It was a communal effort with the plantation furnishing the wood and the tenants the work. Generally, any work that did not involve a tenant working on his own crop was day work for which he was paid. The going rate in 1937 was a dollar a day and these were long days. It wasn't a lot of money but it gave those tenants who were willing to work more a little extra cash. Every Saturday was payday.

* * *

Each tenant was responsible, along with his family members, for his assigned acreage. Of course, my father told him what to do and when to do it and furnished him the mules and plows to work with. The seed and fertilizer were also furnished but charged to the tenant's yearly account.

In addition to working his own plot, the tenant and his family furnished day work labor for the owner's portion of the plantation. There were two tasks connected with cotton when outside labor was often needed: the hoeing and the picking.

Since no chemicals were used, the cotton had to be hoed (or chopped) and plowed quite often to keep the weeds down. The two went together. Every time a field was plowed it was also chopped. If extra hoe hands were needed, my father would send a large farm truck to town. It would be driven slowly through the colored section with the driver blowing the horn. Those who wanted to chop cotton that day (and it was mostly women and children, the men would be already at work) would come running out of the houses with their hoes and climb aboard. Children as young as ten were expected to put in a full day of fieldwork. These extra hands would be paid at the end of each day and brought back to town. The next day the whole process would be repeated.

Extra labor for picking cotton was procured the same way. The main difference was that pay for cotton picking was always by the pound, usually expressed as so much per hundred. In the late 30s a dollar a hundred was standard.

It was backbreaking work dragging a nine-foot canvas sack all day long, not to mention the little burrs on the ends of the cotton bolls which were always pricking the ends of your fingers, breaking off under the skin, festering up, and becoming almost too sore to touch. But good cotton pickers like Junior Potts prided themselves on how many hundred they could get in a day. Junior's goal was to pack his sack with two hundred pounds before noon and to get close to three in the afternoon. The afternoons were longer because you couldn't start picking in the morning until the dew dried off. I remember Junior really getting upset at one noon weigh-in when his sack only tipped the scales at 202 pounds with three knocked off for the sack, giving him only 199 pounds. But Junior and those like him could earn four or five dollars a day picking cotton, a princely sum in those days of a dollar a day for fieldwork.

There were always stories bandied about the picking fields about super pickers who could pick seven or eight hundred pounds a day. They were always "someone I know'd on my las' plantation" or "someone my cousin, Jackie Lee, done hear tell of over 'bout Panther Burn." These were, I'm sure, just embellished tales but they made good listening.

The cotton was weighed-in at noon and again at the end of the day. The sacks were emptied into a small cotton house which stood at the border of the field. Later, it would be transferred to wagons and taken to be ginned.

It was not uncommon to find, especially among the temporary pickers, those who tried to add to their pounds by placing large rocks or horse shoes, or other foreign bodies in their sacks. If caught, they were banished from the fields.

The non-plantation pickers were paid at the end of each day and taken back to town. Tenants were paid on Saturday. Twenty to twenty-five dollars could represent a luxury for the family or a big Saturday night in town.

With the advent of World War II, cotton prices rose and managers worked to increase production. However, the labor supply was diminishing causing the picking price to rise—first to $1.25 per hundred, then to $1.50, and finally $2.00, an exorbitant sum according to the managers. They moaned about the cost of getting the crops picked. But the era of hand-picked cotton was coming to a close as mechanical pickers began to appear in increasing numbers. There was much resistance at first. "Hand-picked cotton is better cotton," avowed many managers. And maybe it was, but with improved technology the steel giants soon took over the cotton fields.

During the time I lived on plantations, "cotton was king." Of course, my father had to raise enough corn, oats and hay to feed the livestock but the owner always wanted every other acre planted in cotton. My father wanted to diversify, especially with soybeans. He argued that soybean prices were always good and could help with the profit margin in years when cotton prices were down as they generally were in the 30s. It was a hard sell. The owners had grown up with cotton, their fathers and grandfathers had built both their plantations and social position on cotton. No need to change a good horse. However, he did manage to get some soybean acreage—until cotton prices began to rise. He, and those few like him, were voices of the future for now soybean acreage in the Delta probably outstrips that of cotton. And diversification has gone to the absurd with catfish farms and gambling casinos.

* * *

There were usually only two white families living on a plantation: the manager's and the owner's who lived in the Big House. All the rest were colored. Although difficult to discern by the casual observer, this group had its own social divisions.

Occupying the top position was the hostler. He usually

had a small family or none at all and his house and garden plot were close to the barns. He was in charge of the feeding and care of the animals (mules, cattle, hogs), of issuing animals and equipment (plows, wagons, harness) to the tenants, of repairing and maintaining the harness, and of seeing that things ran smoothly around the barn lot. Since his was a year-round job, he did not make a crop but was paid a salary.

A notch down from the hostler were those who had some special skills—the tractor drivers and the blacksmith. They might make a small crop if they had a family large enough to work it since most of their time was spoken for during the crop season.

Of all the colored workers, the elite were the servants who worked in the Big House as cooks, maids, butlers, and chauffeurs. There was a sharp line between this group and the majority of coloreds on the place who were generally classified as "field hands" and the "house niggers" were careful to make sure that this line remained sharp. I remember one time being in the yard of the Big House when a "field hand" who was doing some yard work lured one of the maids into the shrubbery and attempted to get under her skirt. She rebuffed him with, "Get yo'self 'way from me, boy. Yo' ain't nothin but a field nigger."

These house positions were much sought after not only for the prestige attached to them but also for the perks. House servants were given leftovers to take home for their family's table. They also were recipients of torn, worn, outdated, or unwanted clothing as well as broken or castoff household items. As a result, they were better fed, better dressed, and had better house furnishing than the common field hand.

There was one hard and fast rule for a house servant: you must not steal from the Big House. Most of the silver items were under lock and key but there were all sorts of other things which could go missing. Mrs. Ganier told the story of a maid she had whose name was Hattie. Hattie always wore a little round hat to work which sat square on top of her head. One evening at quitting time Hattie had her hat on and was going out the back door when Mrs. Ganier stopped her to discuss something they were going to do the next morning. The longer they talked the more Hattie wiped the sweat off her face. It was a warm summer day but Mrs. Ganier thought that the perspiration was somewhat excessive as it quickly soaked the rag Hattie was using. She became more suspicious when she noted that the streams of moisture were not the color of normal sweat and asked Hattie to take off her hat. They had been churning butter that day and there on the top of Hattie's head sat one of the fresh pounds of butter. Hattie was allowed to keep the butter but she was banished from the Big House to spend the rest of her time on that plantation as a field hand.

* * *

Nothing illustrated the similarity of a plantation to a medieval fiefdom any better than the relationship between the plantation and the police. Suffice it to say that the owner and/or his manager were the law on the plantation. No law enforcement person would have come onto a plantation to deal with any of the tenants without first going through the owner or manager. To do so would have been a terrible breach of etiquette.

I remember one Sunday right after dinner a deputy from town came by and told my father that he'd come to arrest Silas for some trouble he'd caused in town the night before. My father got into the car with the deputy and took him down to Silas' house. As they drove up, they saw Silas at the woodpile splitting stove wood. When Silas saw the deputy, he dropped his ax, vaulted a six-foot picket fence, and disappeared into a twenty-acre cornfield. There was no way they were going to find him amongst the eight-foot corn, so the deputy just went on back to town. Later that afternoon my father let me go with him when he got into his pick up and went back to find Silas. He was sitting on the front porch in a straight chair tilted back against the wall. My father did not get out of the truck. He just leaned out the window and commanded, "C'mere, Silas."

Silas ambled out to the truck. "Yasser, Mista Luke."

"Silas, why in the dickens did you run off a while ago? You saw me with the deputy. You knew I wasn't gonna let him hurt you."

"Yasser, Mista Luke, I knows. But my feets jest wudn't stay. When I seen de law, all I seen wuz dat big gun he done had thow'd down on me las' evin' an' deese feets jet tuk me on away."

"Well, Silas, the deputy tells me that you got with some of those boys from over on Sunflower Plantation last night and got into devilment. That right?"

"Yasser, Mista Luke, I ain' gonna lie to ya'. Das whut we done did."

"Well, Silas, we got to go in and take care of it. Get in the back."

Silas started to jump into the bed of the truck but stopped and came back to the window. "Mista Luke, is dey gonna put me in jail?"

"Naw. I'll make bail for you but they've got to arrest you first and you've got to be there for them to do that. After that I'll make your bail and bring you on back."

A look of relief spread over Silas' face. "Thanka, Mista Luke, thanka. I's much obliged to ya'. I knows ya'd take care o' me."

Sometime early on a Sunday morning a deputy would drive out to see my father. "Mr. Boyd, we had to put ol' Dave in jail last night. I know he's one of your tractor drivers and I know you're in the middle of breaking ground for planting, so you're probably gonna need him in the morning. Just come by sometime after dinner and get him." And this my father would do.

During the crop season, the day began about daylight with the ringing of the plantation bell which was mounted on a tall wooden tower next to the barn lot. This was the hostler's job which meant he had to have a clock. Most tenants did not but they did not really need one since their work schedule was governed by the bell. This early morning ringing was the signal for them to get up, come to the barn lot, and get their mules, plows, wagons, and other work equipment. If they were in the middle of plowing time, the plows would have been left in the fields the previous afternoon. This early morning organization usually took from one to two hours since the tenants had to walk varying distances (some as much as a mile and a half) to the barn.

At noon the bell would signal dinner time (not lunch)

and ring everyone back to work at one. At sundown the bell would toll the end of the workday and be followed by the migration of the tenants to the barn with their mules and equipment. One of my favorite tasks in the summer was to ring the bell—the symbol of power and control.

* * *

Perhaps my favorite time of the year was ginning time. Sometime in September the gin men would come and the tin-sided building with all the fascinating machinery would be coaxed back to life after ten months of slumber. Long lines of wagons loaded with cotton would stand waiting their turn to pull under the suction pipe. The cotton would be sucked up into the gin's maw and be routed through a series of machines containing rows of multiple-toothed saws, picks, and other devices. The seeds came out at one place and at the end the white fibers were deposited into a heavy wooden frame. When a particular wagon load was completed, the sides of the frame were moved in, the cotton compressed into a bale, and then secured by steel bands. If these bands were not put on correctly, they could come loose or break when the bale was rolled out of the press turning the cotton into a lethal weapon. Still vivid in my memory is the scene at the press of an exploded bale. It was completely wrapped around a twelve by twelve post which was broken three quarters through. One gin worker had saved himself when he jumped behind the post at the sound of the band's failure.

The gin seemed to take on a life of its own. It was noisy, dusty, and seethed with activity. The gin workers on the inside were always running around yelling at each other over the roar of the machines. Outside, the drivers of the cotton wagons gathered in groups to swap stories. Their ranks were swelled by others on the place who were not otherwise engaged. The cotton platform usually had some activity going on under it. It was built of heavy timbers about six feet off the ground for the deposit of the ginned bales awaiting transport. The main activity for this site was usually a crap game. Every so often some dispute—generally over who had covered the last nickel of the quarter the shooter was betting after he had made his point—would erupt into a fight. Because of this my father discouraged crap games for it they escalated into a cuttin' that meant lost work time with trips to the doctor and incapacitated workers.

Although I was close to some of these, I never felt I was in any danger. When one broke out, one of the tenants would grab me and say something like, "C'mon boy. You ain't got no bizness bein' 'round dis kinda stuff," and hustle me away. I suspected my father had privately assigned two or three of these to watch out for me. Anyway, the last thing any of the combatants would want to happen would be for me to be hurt. Their fate would have been too awful for contemplation.

The worst fracas I ever saw from "under the platform" activities occurred one day right after the dinner break. The wife of one of the gin workers had brought him his dinner but had stayed on to entertain some of the wagon drivers under the cool, dim shade of the platform. Somehow the gin worker got wind of what was going on and interrupted the entertainment. There was yelling and screaming and colored folks flying out from all sides of that platform like chickens from a busted chicken coop.

* * *

Since there were no white children nearby, my father would find my brother and me a little colored boy about our age to play with during the summer when school was out. He would not be able to come every day because even at age seven or eight there were certain jobs he had to do. But two or three days a week were better than nothing. And he loved it—no fieldwork, snacks with Kool-aid, and a peanut butter and jelly sandwich at noon, things he never got at his house. We would dig some worms and go fishing, get the hostler to catch us some mules on which we'd ride around the place, or just play all sorts of games around the barns and sheds.

I remember one summer that LeRoy was our playmate. He had his own set of ideas or superstitions about almost everything and would not accept any counter view. For example, one very hot day we had been playing in the hay loft of the big barn and had come down to the well house to get some water and to cool off. We drank and then let the cool water run over our heads. Gene and I were ready to play some more but LeRoy sat down in the shade of the willow tree that grew by the well house and would not budge. When asked why, he replied, "I cain go out in dat sun wid no wet hed. Hit'l bus' open." We tried to tell him that this wouldn't happen and even stood out in the sun to show that our heads were unaffected. But LeRoy would not be swayed, "Dass cuz yo' hed ain' lik mine. Iffen I's be out dar, my hed 'ud be layin' wide open an' all de brains runnnin' out jus lik' a bussed watermelon. My mama done tol' me dat." So we all just sat there while LeRoy's head recovered.

On another occasion LeRoy told us that he could fly by

just flapping his arms real fast. We challenged him to do so but he said that humans could not just take off from the ground. They had to jump off a high place. When Gene and I scoffed at this, he said, "I'll jes show ya, den." And proceeded to get in our rope swing and pump it up to maximum height which was probably about nine or ten feet. We thought he was just fooling until he launched himself out into space flapping his arms furiously. To his credit LeRoy did not flinch and continued to flap until his face and chest plowed into the ground throwing up a large cloud of dust and knocking the wind out of him. We hauled him over to the well house and threw water on him, which served the dual purpose of washing off the dust and eventually bringing him back to consciousness. "I <u>told</u> you you couldn't fly," I said. His response was not what I expected. "I jest 'bout did. I cud feel m'sef startin' to liff up jest 'fo I hit. I jest needs uh higher place." I looked at LeRoy with muddy water running off him and his nose and lips swelling rapidly from smacking the ground. Then I looked across at the barn loft which was probably thirty feet off the ground and hoped he wouldn't think of tripling his heights and end up killing himself. He <u>knew</u> he could fly under the right conditions; I <u>knew</u> he couldn't. I thought it best to leave it that way. So far as I know, the swing attempt was LeRoy's last "flight."

Except for the colored school in town there was no place for the children on the plantation to attend classes. The town school had short, sporadic sessions but only the town's children lived close enough to attend. There was no bus for the colored children who lived on the plantations. Whites were transported to the white school in town.

Sometimes after the crops were laid by in late summer

and before cotton picking began or in the winter between harvest and spring planting, a teacher might come and hold some classes in the plantation church house. The children might learn a little but not nearly enough.

One day when we were playing with LeRoy, the subject of school came up. He surprised me when he said, "I likes school." I said that I had much rather be fishing, riding mules, or playing in the barn. To which LeRoy observed, "Yeah. But when I ain't in school I's pickin' cotton or toten water to the hoe hands. You ain't." LeRoy might have been ignorant but he wasn't stupid. So much for the doctrine of "separate but equal" in education.

The plantation and the plantation life of the thirties and forties are gone now. Gone also are the tenants and the mules. What few tenant houses that are needed are all clustered around the barns. The others have long since been destroyed. The gooseneck hoes have been replaced by chemicals and the mules have given way to huge machines with enclosed, air conditioned cabs and tape decks. The land still produces cotton and soybeans but the modern delta sports catfish farms and gambling casinos. There was some good in the old but much bad. I suspect the same is true today. The good/bad ratio lies with the one making the assessment. There is, however, one thing for certain. It's different.

07
SAY WHAT?

Sharon was a nurse at the VA hospital. She enjoyed her work with the men who had served their country—and her country, too—and who were still paying a price for this service.

The hospital had some age on it but it was still a good hospital. The only problem was its location. In the 1950s the area surrounding it had been an upscale neighborhood but today it was pretty seedy. Adult bookstores, massage parlors, and dance clubs were so close that their gaudy lights could be seen from any of the rooms. And prostitutes used the adjacent sidewalks as they engaged in the world's oldest profession. Some of these ladies of the evening had become so brazen that they plied their trade during the daylight hours as well. And it was not unusual for them to solicit customers among the staff and patients of the hospital. On more than one occasion, Sharon had to run one of these "girls" out of a patient's room. The mere mention of these streetwalkers caused Sharon to get extremely hot under her starched collar.

It was mid-afternoon and Sharon had just checked in a new patient from a small town in East Tennessee. She walked down to his room to see about him. As she entered, she noted that he was standing at the window in his bathrobe looking down at the street below. She knew what he was looking at. It was a pleasant fall day and the "girls" were out in full force.

Sharon got halfway across the room before he noticed her

and turned around. "I just came by to check on you," she said. "Is there anything else you need?"

"Yes ma'am, there is. I need some ass."

Sharon was shocked—and disappointed. How could this nice looking young man be so brazen? Was he going to pick out one of the "girls" from his window and ask Sharon to go down and close the deal? Or was he just going to send her down to make the selection?

Sharon's shock was rapidly turning into anger which was not helped by the chuckling from the other patient who shared the two-person room. She shot him a withering look but it failed to stop the laughter.

"What did you say you needed?" asked Sharon with a coolness in her voice. She was hoping for a different answer.

"Well, ma'am, I'd just like to have a little ass." The roommate began to laugh harder.

That did it. Sharon was not going to put up with this kind of behavior. He looked to be about the same age as her own son and Sharon determined that what he needed was a good, stern motherly lecture. She moved over and stood beside him at the window. Her voice was businesslike. "My boy, do you realize what kind of women those are down there?"

"Yes ma'am, I sure do."

"Well then, you know they're the dregs of society. Most of 'em are drug addicts and they are carriers of about every kind of sexual disease known to man and beast. And most are HIV positive. They're nothing more than walking death in short, tight skirts. You don't need to be fooling around with any of ‘em”

“Yes ma’am. You’re sure right. And I appreciate you telling me about ‘em. I’m gonna be real careful.” It seemed to Sharon that he was genuinely grateful for her lecture.

“Now, is there anything else I can get you for your room?” Sharon asked.

When his answer came, Sharon turned beet red with embarrassment as she realized why his roommate was still doubled over with laughter.

“Yes ma’am, like I said a minute ago. I need a little ass for my water pitcher.”

08
Would You Do That For Me?

The two young lovers sat on a rock outcropping in a natural alcove beside the rocky trail which clung to the side of the mountain forty or fifty feet above the rushing stream. It and been a tiring hike—and dangerous in places. They sat close together as lovers do. "How far was it from the lodge to the swinging bridge we crossed?' she asked.

He took out the little pamphlet he'd picked up at the front desk on the lodge's trails and consulted it. "Almost a mile and a half."

"Have we come back that far yet?'

"Just about. You can catch a glimpse of the lodge around the bend there."

"And how far is it to that other swinging bridge we'll have to cross to get back on the lodge side?"

"The map shows it about a half mile below the lodge," he replied. Why? Are you tired?"

"A little," she said. "But not too bad." She snuggled her head into his chest. The only sounds were a couple of birds chirping and the tumbling water. Drooping rhododendron limbs practically hid the two from view. "A good hot shower when we get back will fix me up as good as new," she said.

He kissed her on the cheek. Their lips found each other. He slipped a hand under her top and began to fondle one of her breasts. He was glad she was braless. She protested weakly. "What do you think a honeymoon's for?' he asked.

"I'm sure there are some other things but I can't think of any right now," she replied as she slid her hand under his shirt and began to massage his chest.

Their love play continued for several minutes. They were oblivious to the rest of the world. Suddenly and at the same instant, they both became aware of movement on the trail across the stream. The figures seemed strangely out of place. "Good lord!" he exclaimed in a hushed tone. "Is that who I think it is?"

"Yes," she replied. "It's that old couple from the lodge."

They had had dinner with them at the same big table the night before. She had noticed them right away. They were much older than the other guests. The woman was small—not much over five feet with a little hump in her back and wavy white hair. She walked with one of those metal canes with four tips. The man was well over six feet, lean, and ramrod straight. Probably an old military man the girl thought. Not a strand of his straight, white hair was out of place. He was holding her left arm and making sure that she didn't trip over anything. "When we get old, will do you that for me?" the girl whispered to her new husband. "You know I will, " he replied his lips brushing her lightly on the cheek.

As they were getting settled at the table, the old lady had said, "Oh, my goodness. I've forgotten my medicine." Her husband had said, "That's okay, dear. I'll run up and get it," before rushing away.

"When we got old, will you do that for me?" the girl whispered. "Of course, I will," he replied, squeezing her hand under the table.

During table conversation it was revealed that the old couple was celebrating sixty years of marriage. They had always loved the mountains—had spent their honeymoon camping in the mountains. Their children had given them this week at the lodge as an anniversary gift.

During the meal she had trouble buttering her bread. Her husband did it for her. She could not get her meat cut so he did it for her. "When we get old, will you do that for me?" the girl whispered. "You know I will," he whispered back as he playfully stuck his fork into her baked potato.

"What in the world do they think they're doing?" Her husband's words broke into her thoughts. "Surely they saw the big sign at the trailhead."

"They had to," the girl said. "They had to walk around it to get on the trail."

"It said 'Dangerous Trail,' 'Experienced Hikers Only.' And now look at those old fools." The young man seemed exasperated at just how foolish these old people were.

They moved ever so slowly. He practically supported her on one side. The cane in her other hand sparkled in the sunlight. "When we got old, will you do that for me?" she asked. "Of course," he answered without taking his eyes off the old couple.

"Do you remember their name?" she asked. "I think it was kinda odd."

"No. I was giving all my attention to you."

"Fitz something-or-other. Yes, Fitz… Fitz… Fitzwilliam,

I believe."

The old couple halted. They had come to a section that was only wide enough for one person. "Surely they'll turn back now," the young man said. But they didn't. The old man stepped out ahead with one arm stretched out behind holding his wife's hand. "They're gonna kill themselves," the young man said. "I'm gonna yell at them to turn back." He stood and cupped his hand around his mouth to yell but he was too late. The old lady had placed the cane too close to the outside edge and a piece broke away causing her to lose her balance. She gave up her grip on the cane which clattered down the rock face and disappeared into the rushing water. As she fell to her knees, her husband whirled and grabbed her arm with both hands. However, one knee found only air and she rolled over the precipice, pulling him to the ground. The girl was amazed that she hadn't screamed.

The young couple watched the scene in horror. The old woman was kicking both legs and waving her free arm wildly. They heard him say something to her. She stopped struggling and brought her other arm up to clutch one of his. There was no way for the young couple to get to them. He whipped out his cell phone but there was no signal.

The old man struggled to get to his knees so that he would have some leverage but he could not. Finally, he stopped trying. There were no footholds for her on the rock face. Both couples knew it was only a matter of time. The young man could not pull his eyes away. They felt as if they had been glued in their sockets. The girl began to cry.

A calm seemed to come over the old couple. The young

couple could see that they were talking to each other. They could see their grips weakening as she slipped lower and lower. Finally, she turned her face up toward his. He said something and his lips formed a kiss. They knew that hers were doing the same. Suddenly, their hands separated and she plunged into the water. She came struggling to the surface. The young man thought she might be able to grab a tree branch or vine but such was not the case. The cold water sucked her under as she passed around the bend and out of sight.

The old man lay with his arms and head dangling over the edge for a minute or two. Then, he struggled to his knees and put his face in his hands. It was obvious that he was crying. The young couple stared transfixed. Finally, he dropped his hands to his thighs and stood up straight on his knees his eyes fixed on the water. Slowly, he began to lean toward the river.

When she realized what he was doing, the girl jumped up to shout, "NO! NO! DON'T DO IT!" but the words balled up in her throat like a large wad of phlegm. At some point gravity took over and pulled him out into space. He turned over once and hit the water feet first. He did not struggle as his wife had but gave himself to the stream's watery embrace. Only one arm reappeared above the surface and then he was gone.

The young couple stood looking at the water for a long time. The birds continued to chirp. Finally, they turned to face each other. Her eyes asked, "Would you do <u>that</u> for me?" His eyes did not answer.

09
THE REVIVAL

It was the third week in August—always the most important week of the year for the East Fork Southern Missionary Baptist Church. Ever since anyone could remember, the Church's Revival Meeting had been held during that week and this year was no exception. Each service started at 7:00 o'clock and ended when the visiting evangelist decided that the sinners on the mourners' bench had been prayed over enough and that further altar calls were unlikely to produce more respondents. The latest closing time was 11:10 on a Saturday night in 1927. Old-time members still talked about the shouting, speaking in tongues, and other manifestations of the Spirit on that particular evening. Most avowed that they'd "probably never see anything like that again."

The Meeting always started on Sunday evening and ended the following Saturday. This allowed the visiting preacher to conduct the services and not be absent from his home pulpit. This year's services were being led by Reverend Ossie Tidford who pastored two half-time churches over close to Cedartown. Reverend Sunday James, East Fork's pastor, had come to know Reverend Tidford through the Area Association of Ministers and had been impressed with his animated style. It would be safe to say that no one could sleep during one of Brother Ossie's sermons.

Reverend Tidford liked to conduct these revivals and was in great demand in the several surrounding counties.

Brother Ossie's preaching could be classified as animated in his home churches. In a Meeting it was known to reach unimagined heights. Yes, Reverend James had done a good day's work when he persuaded Reverend Ossie Tidford to come for East Fork's August Meeting.

The food was another reason Reverend Tidford enjoyed these engagements. He and his wife were usually lodged with a different family each day, none of which spared on quality or quantity at mealtime.

And the money wasn't bad either. Reverend Tidford had no set fee for his services but he had found that the more he moved the congregation's spirit the wider they opened their purses. On a good week, he would head for home on Saturday evening with as much as one hundred dollars cash money in his pocket.

The East Fork Meeting got off to a good start. Reverend James had taken a week of vacation from the chicken plant in Maynardville to help with the daily visiting. Except for a bountiful midday meal with a designated family, each day was spent visiting church members as well as those who were in need of being saved. Brother Ossie was very persuasive and that combined with the word-of-mouth descriptions of his fiery sermons resulted in capacity crowds. By the close of the service on Wednesday, there were six candidates for baptism with more expected. Reverend James would do the actual baptizing on the next preaching Sunday.

The Thursday night service was even better (and longer) than the previous four. So many wanted to come to the mourners' bench that they had to do so in shifts. When the evening was over, there were two more candidates for baptism, several rededications, and a whole bunch of sins and indiscretions confessed from the mourners' bench. Some of the latter were a surprise and some shocked the congregation. A surprise and shock because no one in the community was aware of them. As old Miz Effie Mae Udell said after the service, "You can tell the Spirit's working when folks confess to sins nobody knows about." And even greater things were predicted for Friday. One or two even dared to mention the breaking of the 11:10 record but in hushed tones as if they were speaking about the breaking of some sacred, God-given law.

And Friday night fulfilled all the predictions and then some. Brother Ossie hit his stride early in the evening and never looked back. The mourners' bench filled early and often with new shocking revelations. Old Deacon Mooneyham began to speak in tongues and did so for at least half an hour inspiring two other deacons to join him. Two or three women began to shout.

All of this was too much for fifteen-year-old Lacy Sue Haycraft whose eyes rolled back in her head as she pitched forward off the mourners' bench and began to roll about the front of the church. Her tumblings caused her to assume about every position her body was capable of. In her state she was unaware of the location of her skirt which migrated quickly to the north exposing most of her lower body to public scrutiny. Since the hot August weather called for a minimum of undergarments, Lacy Sue put on quite a show. Several of the teenage boys were quick to note this and rushed forward to the mourners' bench for a better view. There was not room for them all so some had to stand behind the bench. Quite unaware of what was taking place on the floor behind him as he prayed over those on the mourners' bench, Brother Ossie turned his pleas up a notch or two when he saw this rush of young people. This caused additional affirmation from the congregation which, in turn, sent the good Reverend to even greater heights.

After what seemed like an eternity, Reverend Tidford realized what was happening as three ladies of the Church rushed forward, held Lacy Sue down, and got her clothing back in order and her back to reality. Somewhat shakened by this turn of events, he pulled back and, within a few minutes, brought the service to a close. Brother Ossie knew that he could have gone on but somehow, he just didn't feel as if it was proper to do so. Anyway, they had had a good night: four new candidates for baptism, over twenty rededications, and many heretofore-unknown sins confessed. The clock read 10:37. The talk about a record-breaking Saturday night increased.

The Tidfords were scheduled to spend that evening with the Stoddards. Brother Tidford and Brother James had visited the family earlier in the week giving special attention to Nellie Jean, the Stoddards seventeen-year-old daughter. Other church members were concerned with her spiritual condition, as were the Stoddards. She was known to run with a fast crowd and had even been seen frequenting some of the local dances. However, Nellie Jean did not seem to have the same concern as her family and neighbors. In response to Brother Ossie's pleas for her to "join up with the Lord," Nellie Jean replied, "Brother Tidford, I'm having too good of a time. Anyway, I just don't hear the Lord calling me." Somewhat taken aback by her frankness, Brother Ossie replied, "You'd best be careful, Nellie Jean. Sometimes the Devil comes for those who don't listen for the Lord's call." Brother Ossie did not realize at the time just how prophetic his words would prove to be.

The Stoddards lived in a big old, rambling farmhouse. It had several dormers in both the main roof and the roof of the rear ell which provided light and ventilation to the upstairs bedrooms. The Tidfords were shown to a bedroom upstairs in the ell.

As they were preparing for bed, Brother Ossie poured some water from the pitcher into the large bowl on the washstand and began sponging himself off with a washcloth. "You know, Alene, what I'd like right now mor'in anything? A bath. We haven't stayed in a place with an indoor bathroom all week. I feel like I'm all scabbed over with dirt. These spit baths help a little but you know how hard I've been preaching and visiting. Yes, if the Lord wanted to send me something, He could start with a full tub of water and a bar of Lifebouy soap."

You're right," Alene replied, "I could use one myself. But we've just got one more day. We can both have a good washing tomorrow night."

"Yes," mused Ossie, "a good bath. I'd like to smell good when I break that 1927 time record tomorrow night."

"What do you mean when <u>you</u> break the record?" There was an edge in Alene's voice.

"That's what I mean. I've been close the last two nights and coulda done it either one. But that woulda left nothing to look forward to. No, the last night's the night to do it."

"Don't you think the Lord might have something to say about it?" Alene seemed a little more disturbed.

"Well, I'm sure the Lord won't mind for His hard-working servant to get some benefits. Just think of the responses I've already gotten this week. And when word gets around about this record, there's just no telling how many more invitations will come in. Why, I might go statewide and get to doing nothing but revival meetings."

"But, how can you be so sure you can do it?" Alene was skeptical as well as apprehensive.

"Aw, Alene, you've been in all the services. I've got these folks eating out of my hand and I'm gonna take 'em to the limit tomorrow night. Just you wait and see."

Well, maybe you will, Ossie. But I don't feel good about it. Dry yourself off and come on to bed."

The thunder and the sound of rain on the tin roof awakened Alene sometime in the middle of the night. She sat upright when she realized that Ossie was not in bed with her. The flashes of lightning revealed him standing at one of the open, screenless windows. "What's wrong, Ossie?" she asked, her mind still clouded with sleep.

"Nothing's wrong, dear," answered Ossie without turning around, "hand me that towel and soap. The Lord has done sent a bath shower."

Alene was suddenly wide-awake. "What in the world are you gonna do?"

"Why, I'm gonna sit right out on this little ledge and get myself cleaned up. It'd be a shame to waste the Lord's water after He's done sent it," Ossie replied as he shucked off his nightshirt and climbed out the window.

Alene jumped out of bed, grabbed the soap and towel from the washstand, and handed the soap to her husband. "I wish you wouldn't do this. What if somebody sees you?"

"Who in the world you think is gonna be out in the middle of nowhere in the dead of night in a thunderstorm?"

Brother Ossie worked up a good lather over most of his body holding each arm aloft in turn as he gave special attention to its armpit. It felt especially good when he held both arms up and threw his head back and let the warm August rain run the length of his body. He even laughed with the joy of it all.

"Please be quiet, Ossie," cautioned Alene as she stood holding the towel and biting her trembling lower lip. "Somebody's gonna hear you."

Ossie replied by throwing his head back to laugh again while lifting one leg to give it a good soaping. However, he had miscalculated the narrowness of the ledge and just how slick a wet, soapy tin roof could be. In a flash of lightning, Alene saw him throw both arms up as if grasping for some nonexistent support and disappear into the night.

She stood stunned for a few seconds before springing into action. Guided by lightning flashes, Alene bolted out the door, through the hall, and down the back stairs. She slowly pushed open the door to the side porch and peeked out into the stormy night. She saw nothing at first but in the flashes she thought she could see a leg sticking out of one of the large boxwoods that bordered the porch. "Is that you, Ossie?" she asked timidly.

"Good Lord, woman, who else do you think would be out here!" exclaimed Ossie as he struggled to extricate himself from the clutches of the boxwood.

"Are you hurt?" Alene came out on the porch.

"No. I'm OK. This bush is a little prickly, but it broke my fall," replied Ossie as he scrambled to his feet and climbed up on the porch.

Alene wrapped the towel around him. "Come on. Let's get you back upstairs before someone sees us," she urged.

Just as they got to the door Ossie realized that he had mud all over his feet. "Just a minute. Let me wash my feet off so I don't track up the house." He went back and sat down on the edge of the porch and stuck his feet out under the drip. With the amount of water that was running off the house, it didn't take long to get them clean.

They got back to their room without being seen. Ossie got dried off and some lotion on the scratches on his buttocks and upper torso. As they climbed back into bed, he declared that he felt cleaner than he had in a long time. "Yes, the Lord's rain is a cleansing rain," declared Ossie. The remainder of the night was uneventful.

Brother Ossie took Saturday afternoon off from visiting to rest up for what he anticipated would be a tiring service. The events of the evening proved him correct.

The church house was packed with a few even standing around the back wall. Brother Ossie started slowly. No sense in peaking too early; he had a long way to go.

It was a warm evening and as Brother Ossie became increasingly more animated, he began to sweat profusely.

He took off his coat and laid it aside. Sometime later his tie followed the coat. The intensity increased; the mourners' bench filled again and again; there were several shocking confessions; people were jumping up and down and shouting all over the room; Deacon Mooneyham's speech went into tongues again. The service seemed to take on a life of its own.

Along about 10:30 Brother Ossie loosened his cuffs and pushed his sleeves up as far as they would go. As he prayed and preached in front of the mourners' bench, he began to wave his arms above his head and throw his head back. Perspiration streamed down his face. He was as wet as he had been on the Stoddard's roof in the storm.

Nellie Jean Stoddard was sitting on the back row with several of her friends. Brother Ossie's wet face, thrown back head, and flailing arms brought a flashback that she could not ignore. She rushed forward weeping and shouting, "I've got to testify, Brother Ossie, I've got to testify!"

"Speak on sister," encouraged Ossie as he turned her around to face the congregation.

"You was right, Brother Ossie. The Devil does come for folks. He come for me last night and I seen him!"

"Tell it, Nellie Jean, tell it!" said Ossie.

"Yes sir, I seen him! He was a' sittin out on my roof in the storm! He was naked and waving his bony arms around and throwing his head back and laughing and then he was gone! But I know he was there 'cause this morning we saw his muddy footprints on our side porch and where he'd tore up one of our boxwoods!"

Nellie Jean's testimony brought Ossie back to reality. "That's good, Nellie Jean, that's good. Thank you, thank you for those words."

"But I ain't through, Brother Ossie, I want to tell everybody what he looked like. He was fearsome looking with froth and foam running all off him...."

Ossie cut her off. "There's no use describing him, Nellie Jean. He can take on so many forms and anyway, this is the Lord's service and there's just no reason to be concentrating on the Devil." With that he got her quiet and seated.

The congregation could see that Ossie was visibly shaken but they would never have guessed the reason. He closed the service out in short order before Nellie Jean could get started again. The clock read 10:58.

After the service everybody had to come by and shake Brother Ossie's hand and tell him what a wonderful week it had been. Miz Effie Mae Udell said, "The '27 service might have been longer but it wasn't no better. And second place ain't nothing to be ashamed of."

As the Tidfords headed for home, Ossie drove for several miles over the gravel road before Alene broke the silence. "Well?"

"Eighteen saved, forty-three rededications, and a whole bunch of confessions," responded Ossie.

"That's not what I'm asking."

"One hundred and twenty-seven dollars," Ossie replied.

"That's not it either. What I really want to know is did you learn a lesson tonight?"

"I shore did, dear, I shore did."

"Well?"

After a long pause, Ossie responded, "Both the Lord and the Devil work in mysterious ways."

10
A MATTER OF HEART

Bernice deserves to die. Yes, thought Sarah Lou as she backed out of her driveway, if anybody deserves to die, she does. A person who would just kill four people—Sarah Lou knew of four for sure, there could be more—did not deserve to live. It should have only been three but the poor little State Farm Insurance man had gotten in the way, been at the wrong place at the wrong time, was just trying to do his job and be of service. He'd left a young widow and two small children but Bernice didn't seem to care. She had to be stopped—stopped before she claimed more victims. Sarah Lou hoped her plan would work and that she'd be able to pull it off. She had to for the sake of her brother Cory, who'd died along with the State Farm man. Just the thought of him gave her more resolve. She turned the car toward the interstate.

* * *

Nothing had been the same since she'd come to town. From somewhere in Arkansas, she claimed. She wasn't very clear about her past. She didn't seem to lack for money. Said her husband had died and left her well fixed. She'd bought the old Simpson place and fixed it up sparing no expense. Folks said her late husband had left her <u>very</u> well fixed. Folks also heard the rumors that even the Big River couldn't stop—rumors that she'd had not one but two husbands to die under suspicious circumstances. Now here she was in Rosedale. Folks wondered why. The answer was not long in coming.

It was obvious that she'd set her cap for Cory MacIntyre right from the first. Cory had never been married and Bernice just swept him off his feet. In about six months she had him hooked and landed. And before they celebrated their first anniversary the tragedy occurred.

It was a day about like any other day. The farmers were trying to get their cotton and bean crops in. As a consequence, the hardware store was busy and Cory didn't get home for supper until after seven o'clock. Bernice had prepared a good meal. She was a good cook. In spite of all the bad things the townfolks said about her, they had to give her that. And she had fixed Cory's favorite dessert, blackberry cobbler with a topping of vanilla ice cream. Just as she was getting ready to serve it, Petey Bledsoe, the State Farm agent, stopped by with the new policies on all Cory's vehicles. Cory insisted that he sit down with them and have some dessert. He agreed and Bernice dished up two bowls and put them before the men. "Aren't you having any, honey?" Cory asked.

"No, not tonight," Bernice replied. "You didn't marry a fat woman and I don't want to become one. You boys just eat your desserts and go on in the den and talk business. I'll clean up the kitchen."

While she was engaged in this chore, Bernice heard some unusual noises from the den. There was a loud thump like a piece of furniture being overturned followed by a series of lesser thumps like a person's heels being kicked against the floor. She did not go to investigate before running all the leftovers including the remainder of the cobbler down the garbage disposal and turning on the dishwasher. When she got to the den, both men were on the floor turning blue and barely moving. She grabbed the phone and called 911.

Sarah Lou, Bernice, and Petey's wife were at the hospital. They had just been taken into a separate room and informed by the doctor that both men were dead—both from cardiac arrest as best as he could tell. As the doctor left, Sheriff Billy Dick Spencer came in. "Ladies, I'm sorry for your losses." Then, he stumbled over a few words before continuing apologetically, "Considering the circumstances of the deaths, the law requires autopsies. You won't be able to plan funerals until they're done. I'm sure sorry about this."

Only Bernice spoke. "You don't need to apologize, Sheriff. We know you're just doing your job."

"Thank you kindly ma'am for understanding," replied Billy Dick. "By the way, Miss Bernice, while it's fresh on your mind, did anything unusual happen that might have caused this?"

"No, why no, Sheriff," responded Bernice, in a trembly voice between dabs of her eyes with a tissue. "Cory just came in from work and we had supper. As we were finishing, Mr. Bledsoe came by with Cory's new policies. We all had some blackberry cobbler and then the men went into the den to talk business while I cleaned up. Before I got through, I heard a funny noise and went into the den and found them."

"That's very clear, ma'am," replied Billy Dick as he jotted down her statement.

"Almost too clear," thought Sarah Lou. She'd never liked Bernice. Even in her shock at the death of her brother, something just didn't feel right.

A week or so later the report came back—both men, cardiac arrest.

* * *

A few days after the burial reality began to set in for Sarah Lou. Bernice had inherited everything Cory owned—the house, the vehicles, the farm, his stocks as well as the pay off from his half million dollar life insurance policy. The only thing she didn't get was the hardware store. Sarah Lou and Cory were partners and the partnership agreement provided that in the event one died, the store went to the surviving partner.

Sarah Lou was in the store one afternoon after school talking to Ferguson. He'd assisted Cory for a number of years and Sarah Lou had hired him to manage the store for her. Bernice came walking in.

"What in the world does she want?" thought Sarah Lou. "Probably wants to see if she can't get the store along with everything else." It was also unusual to see Bernice in the store. In fact she hadn't been inside since the wedding. Said she didn't like the smell of it, that it was a man's store.

They exchanged greetings; Sarah Lou's was cool but Bernice didn't seem to notice. She spoke in a smooth syrupy voice. "I just thought I'd come down and get Cory's personal things from the office and save you the trouble of having to go through them."

There was something about Bernice's manner that raised a warning flag in Sarah Lou's mind. She had already concluded that Bernice had killed her only brother. She just hadn't been able to figure out how she did it. When she responded, her voice was firm. "No, that won't be necessary. There's a lot of family stuff in there. I'll go through it when I get a chance and send you anything you ought to have. Anyway, I wouldn't want you to have to do this while you're still grieving." Sarah Lou's tone bordered on sarcasm. There had to be something in the office Bernice wanted and Sarah Lou intended for it to stay there until she figured out what it was.

"Oh, but I insist on doing it," replied Bernice sweetly.

"No, I insist that you not do it. I'll tend to it in due time." Sarah Lou spoke more firmly.

"Well, all right, my dear." Honey still dripped from every word. "But if you change your mind, just call."

"I'll be sure to do that."

As Bernice left, Sarah Lou turned to Ferguson, "Don't let that woman near that office. And if she tries again, call me and let me know."

"I sure will, Miss MacIntyre. You can count on her not bothering anything around here." Obviously, Ferguson had no love for Bernice and Sarah Lou knew he'd keep Cory's things secure until she figured out what Bernice wanted.

The next day at school Sarah Lou found a note in her mailbox to call Ferguson at the store. He reported that Bernice had indeed been in again that morning wanting access to the office. Ferguson had turned her away.

The next day Sarah Lou got another phone call from Ferguson. He said that Bernice had come by while he was on his lunch hour but he'd left specific instructions with Burt who wouldn't let her in either. Ferguson ended with, "If she comes around here again, I'm just likely to throw her butt out in the street."

Sarah Lou had to smile. "Just do what you have to do."

Yes, there was something in Cory's office that Bernice wanted. Sarah Lou had looked around it two or three times and seen nothing obvious. The important thing was to keep whatever it was there until she figured out what it was.

* * *

A couple of days later Sarah Lou dropped by the Sheriff's office on her way home from school. She had known Billy Dick Spencer for many years. In fact, he had been one of her senior English students at Rosedale High. He had not been as good an English student as he had been a football player, but he was no dummy. She thought he'd been a good sheriff.

He ushered her into his office, closed the door, offered her a seat, and sat down behind his desk. "Well, Miss Sarah, what brings you down here? Is there something I can do for you?"

Sarah Lou came directly to the point. "I want to know what you're going to do about that woman. You know she killed Cory and Petey both."

"You mean Miss Bernice."

"Why, of course, I mean Bernice. How could two healthy men, one in his forties and the other in his twenties, both suffer cardiac arrest at the same instance in the same house? That goes against all odds not to mention common sense."

"Yes ma'am, you're right, but I can't prove that. . . ."

Sarah Lou cut him off, "You mean you don't think she

did it? That goes against all reason. . ."

Billy Dick interrupted, "Wait a minutes, Miss Sarah. I didn't say what I thought. I said I couldn't prove." He sat back in his chair and looked at the ceiling obviously mulling something over in his mind. He leaned forward and fixed her with a penetrating gaze. "Normally, I wouldn't say this to anybody about an investigation but you were one of my best teachers and I always found you to be a straight shooter. And you've got to promise me that you won't breathe a word of this to anyone."

"I promise, Billy Dick."

"Okay, I'm going to tell you exactly what I think. I think she poisoned both of 'em. I think she used something exotic that leaves no trace and produces cardiac arrest. I think it was in the blackberry cobbler because that was the only common food in both their stomachs. I don't think Bernice ate any of it like she said but the only way to prove that was to have her stomach pumped that night which we didn't know at the time and couldn't have done legally even if we had. And there was no evidence in the kitchen with all the leftovers down the garbage disposal and the dishes run through the dishwasher. Yes ma'am, that's what I think—but I can't prove any of it."

"What about the rumors about her earlier husbands in Arkansas. Maybe you could make a trip over there and find out something that would help." Sarah Lou was grasping at straws.

"I don't need to go to Arkansas. I've been in touch with the folks over there. She's left two dead husbands in two different towns and both died from cardiac arrest. That increases the odds but doesn't prove what we need to prove."

The Sheriff had been more thorough than Sarah Lou figured. He was obviously doing all he could do. "I'm sorry, Billy Dick, I'm just frustrated at knowing what we can't prove. I hear she's putting the farm up for sale next week. I'm afraid she's going to liquidate everything and be gone before we can stop her."

"Yes ma'am, I'm afraid of the same thing. That's why I'm keeping a close watch on her. But my hands are tied unless she does something illegal or I can get some proof about Cory and Petey."

Sarah Lou left Billy Dick's office feeling infuriated and defeated. There had to be a way—what was it?

* * *

The next week Sarah Lou was going into her doctor's office for her regular check-up when she bumped into Bernice who was just leaving. They spoke but did not stop to talk.

As she was signing in at the desk, she overheard her doctor say to the receptionist, "Make an appointment for Mrs. MacIntyre with Dr. Rogers in Jackson as soon a you can get one and call her and tell her when it is."

Sarah Lou recognized the doctor's name. He was a heart specialist who had treated her mother before she died. So, Bernice had a heart condition. How ironic.

* * *

It was seafood buffet night at the Rosedale Country Club and Sarah Lou was there with her sister Christine. She ran into Frank Coldtharp, the Vice President of the Farmer's Home Bank, in the buffet line. After a couple of polite exchanges, Frank remarked, "I always thought your sister-in-law was real nice, but she nearly ate me up a week or so ago."

"Bernice? What in the world for?"

"Well, she came down to the bank wanting last month's statement. Said she hadn't received it. I explained to her that Cory had been in the bank the day before he died and we had all the statements laid out ready to mail, so I just handed his to him. That really upset her. Said she kept track of all the accounts and it was irresponsible of me not to mail it to her. I told her it was a joint account and Cory had just as much right to it as she did. I got her another copy of it but she wanted all the canceled checks. Said Cory never got home with them. I've never seen a woman so upset over a few checks when the account was in good order."

"Thank you for letting me know that, Frank," Sarah Lou replied. Something had clicked in her head.

* * *

Sarah Lou left the buffet and went to the hardware store. The bank statement had to be what Bernice wanted. She looked through Cory's desk and through the stuff stacked on top. No bank statement. What could he have done with it? She leaned back in the desk chair and looked around the small room. There would have been no need for him to hide it. Then, her eyes fell on one of his jackets hanging on the coat rack in the corner. Cory had always been bad about sticking things in his pockets and forgetting about them. She jumped up and snatched the jacket off its hook. There in an inside pocket were two letters he was supposed to have mailed—and the bank statement.

It had been opened. Cory had gone through it. With trembling hands Sarah Lou pulled the statement from the envelope. The canceled checks were all loose except one which had a note clipped to it which said, "Ask Bernice about this." It was a check for $783.50 made out Picchu Pharmaceuticals of Peru and signed by Bernice. Maybe this was the smoking gun.

Sarah Lou sped home her heart racing. She ran to her computer and in a few minutes found the company's web site. They promised absolute confidentiality and advertised a complete line of drugs, including exotic poisons. She requested a catalog.

When it came, it only took her a few minutes to find the only poison listed that caused cardiac arrest within thirty minutes and was undetectable in the body after an hour. As a final check, she figured the shipping charges and added them to the listed price. The total came to $783.50. Sarah Lou had, indeed, found the smoking gun.

The next day she took the catalog and check to Billy Dick. He looked them over carefully and then tilted back in his chair and looked at the ceiling in deep thought. Finally, Sarah Lou broke the silence. "Are you going to arrest her?"

Billy Dick's chair came down. "No ma'am, I'm not."

Sarah Lou was outraged, "Why not? You've got the proof right there."

"No, Miss Sarah." Bill Dick's voice was calm and even. "What I've got are a couple more pieces to the puzzle and I'm gonna check with ole Jim Tom down at the post office. He'll remember mail coming through from Peru. But there're still too many holes and a smart lawyer—and believe me Bernice will have a smart one—will find all of 'em and probably some nobody's even thought about. Just for instance, there're probably some more things in this catalog that would total $783.50 and we can't prove she didn't order one of those. And we can't prove she didn't eat any of the blackberry cobbler. What we've got is some circumstantial evidence, a lot of coincidences, and a very smart woman. The DA is not about to try a case he won't win. If he did and she were acquitted, double jeopardy would come into play and she'd be home free on both Cory and Petey"

"Then you're not going to do anything." There was a note of disgust in Sarah Lou's voice.

"I didn't say that. I'm gonna do everything I can do legally. I'm gonna put these items in the file. I'm gonna check at the post office. I'm gonna watch Bernice like a hawk. But she's not the type to slip up much."

Sarah Lou was silent for a time. "Okay, then, but I want copies of the check and the catalog." Billy Dick got up and made them himself. Sarah Lou put the items away in her purse. "You know what would serve her right?"

"What?"

"For her to suffer the same fate as her four victims."

Billy Dick looked startled. "Don't do anything foolish, Miss Sarah. You know I couldn't cut you any slack."

Sarah Lou rose to leave. "I know. And I wouldn't expect you to. Let's stay in touch on this."

Billy Dick sat looking at the ceiling for a long time thinking about the facet of his former teacher he'd not seen before.

* * *

Bernice became an obsession with Sarah Lou. She could not get her out of her mind—and how to stop the woman and make her pay for all the evil she'd done. Sarah Lou conceived and rejected several plans. Frustration was beginning to set in. Then, out of the blue an answer came.

One evening Sarah Lou was reviewing the works of Edgar Allen Poe in preparation for a unit she was doing with her English classes when all the pieces she'd been fumbling with fell into place. There it was—a plan that seemed to spring from that master of the macabre himself. Mr. Poe would be proud of her.

* * *

In the next few days, Sarah Lou visited most of the eating places around town. There weren't that many. Her plan had to have the proper setting. She settled on the "County Cafeteria" out at the interstate.

Sarah Lou was glad she'd never accused Bernice to her face of poisoning Cory. That made it easier to persuade her to meet for lunch "just to give some closure about Cory's death." Sarah Lou had picked a time just before the lunch time rush.

Ahead Sarah Lou could see the tall signs that marked the

interstate businesses. She took a deep breath and steeled herself for what she was about to do.

* * *

Sarah Lou made sure that Bernice went through the line first. She was also careful to pick the same food items Bernice did. When they came to the dessert section, Sarah Lou exclaimed, "Would you believe it, Bernice!? They have blackberry cobbler, Cory's favorite dessert. Let's have some as we remember him." Over Bernice's weak protests, Sarah Lou put a dish of cobbler on both trays saying, "I know you like it, too."

Sarah Lou guided Bernice to a booth in a little alcove that jutted off the main dining area. It was out of the view of the serving line and rather secluded with the ladies room on one side and a beverage serving station on the other. Sarah Lou made sure that Bernice got her tray emptied and seated first. As she finished putting her items on the table, Sarah Lou carelessly sat a glass of water down on the end of the napkin rolled silverware. It turned over and dumped its contents into Bernice's lap. She apologized profusely and tried to dry Bernice's skirt off with her napkin. Bernice jumped up with an angry exclamation and ran around the corner to the ladies room to do a proper job. Mr. Poe could not have done better.

The meal was rather strained to say the least. As Bernice was finishing her cobbler, Sarah Lou took the copy of the drug catalog out of her bag and laid it on the table in front of her. She turned pale, "Wh-what's this?" she stammered, visibly shaken.

"You know very well what it is. I know what you did,

what you used, and how much it cost," replied Sarah Lou as she flipped open the pages and pointed to the entry circled in red.

Bernice fought to regain her composure. "You can't prove anything."

"You're right," said Sarah Lou as she sat back in her chair with a gloating look on her face. "But the beautiful thing is I don't have to." She looked at her watch, "I figure you've got a little less than thirty minutes."

"Don't try to con me," responded Bernice with an obvious sneer, "There's nothing could be put in a person's food in a cafeteria line. You're just trying to shake me. . . ." Suddenly a look of horror came on her face as she remembered. . . "The water!" Her voice was barely a whisper. "You were here with my food."

"That's right. You think my dumping my water in your lap was an accident? Surely you of all people can recognize a good plan."

Large beads of sweat popped out on Bernice's forehead. She began to gasp for air. "You couldn't."

"Oh yes I could."

Now Bernice's whole body was drenched with sweat. She struggled to focus her eyes.

"You had the poison in Cory's blackberry cobbler. I thought the same for you would be a nice touch. Rather poetic, don't you think?"

"Help me!" croaked Bernice as her legs and arms began to grow numb.

"You know you're beyond help now. Just like Cory and the State Farm man."

Bernice's face began to turn blue. Her lips moved but no words came out. She pitched forward amongst the dirty dishes and then flopped backward and slid under the table. Sarah Lou jumped up and screamed.

Then the chaos began. People came from all directions to help. Sirens of the approaching emergency vehicles grew louder. Billy Dick was in the room within minutes. He ordered all their dirty dishes held for evidence. She heard him talking to Doc Stone's office on his cell. He was the County Coroner. "I don't care if he's at lunch, on the golf course, or seeing patients, you tell him there's a body on the way. Tell him to get it in the autopsy room immediately. Time is critical. I'll be there in ten minutes to tell him what to look for."

Sarah Lou was sitting calmly in a booth across the room. Billy Dick came over. "Miss Sarah, I sure hope you haven't gone and done something foolish." She just shrugged her shoulders. "Please don't plan on leaving town."

"Why, Bill Dick, I'm not going anyplace. Rosedale's my home."

He just looked at her accusingly. "I'll be in touch," he said before turning on his heel and heading for the hospital.

* * *

Sarah Lou went about her normal routine as well as she

could while waiting for the sheriff's call. She knew what she was going to face and wanted to get it over with. After a week and no call, Sarah Lou thought to herself, "Billy Dick's playing some mind game hoping I'll break or do something stupid. He's gonna have to wait a long time for that to happen." The call finally came at the end of the second week and again she found herself sitting in front of Billy Dick's desk. He clasped and unclasped his hands as he tried to figure out where to begin. After what seemed like an eternity to Sarah Lou, he began.

"Miss Sarah, you know what I'm thinking just as well as I do. You remember the first time you came to me about Bernice and I sort of laid my cards on the table?"

"Yes, I do. Are you going to arrest me?"

"I'll come to that in due time. But first, I'm gonna lay out my cards. I've talked to everybody I know to talk to and checked everything I know to check. I started out with the premise that you poisoned Bernice with the same stuff from the same source she used on Cory and Petey. Jim Tom remembers Bernice sending a letter to Peru, Bernice getting a package from Peru, and you getting the catalog from Peru. But he doesn't recall any other traffic between you and Peru."

"Maybe I used another post office," suggested Sarah Lou almost tauntingly.

"No you didn't because I've checked every post office within a fifty mile radius. None have had any Peru traffic. Besides, you haven't been out of town or even mailed a letter since that day you brought that check and catalog in."

"How do you know . . . .Billy Dick, have you been having

me watched?"

"I sure have, you and Bernice both. How do you think I got to the cafeteria so quick? And another thing, I've checked your bank account and credit card transactions. Nothing has gone to Peru."

"Maybe I used cash." Sarah Lou was beginning to enjoy this game.

"If you did, you had it in a sock someplace. You've only withdrawn small amounts of cash. Even then, how did you get it down there? I don't think they have a carrier pigeon service."

"I'll have to give it to you, Billy Dick. You were always a thorough student and you still are. But what about the autopsy?"

"I was coming to that. What do you think it showed?"

Sarah Lou made hard eye contact as she answered, "Cardiac arrest."

"You're right. We beat the catalog's deadline by at least thirty minutes and the poison didn't show up. Nothing either on the dishes. All Doc Stone could come up with was cardiac arrest?"

"Maybe she had some sort of heart condition," suggested Sarah Lou.

"She did," responded Billy Dick, "but the doctor says it wouldn't have killed her by itself unless something triggered it and made it more severe than it was. Did you notice anything unusual.

"No. Nothing that stands out."

Billy Dick was looking at the ceiling again. Suddenly he leaned forward over his desk and pinned Sarah Lou's eyes with his, "Miss Sarah, you were one of the best teachers I ever had. In addition to English you taught us about honor, honesty, integrity, truthfulness, and all sorts of things like that. Now, I'm going to ask you one question." He leaned even closer and Sarah steeled herself for what she knew was coming. "Did you poison Bernice?"

Their eyes were locked together. Sarah Lou struggled not to blink, not to avert her eyes, and to keep her voice steady. "No, Billy Dick, I did not."

She felt as if Billy Dick's gaze went straight through into her brain. After what seemed like an eternity, he broke it off, leaned back in his chair, and looked at the ceiling. "Thank you, Miss Sarah. I'm sorry that you've had to go through all this. I won't bother you with it again." He seemed almost satisfied. But after several seconds he continued, "I've got nothing but dead ends. I've got three heart deaths in a very short time span and all the victims are connected. That's just too much of a coincidence for me to buy. Now, Miss Sarah, I somehow get the feeling that you know a lot more about this than I do. What would you say killed Bernice?"

Sarah Lou paused for several seconds as if she were trying to decide just what to say or whether to say anything at all. Billy Dick watched her closely. Finally, she spoke. "Billy Dick, do you remember when you were in my classes and we studied Edgar Allen Poe?"

"Why, yes, I do, Miss Sarah."

"Well, I'm sure Mr. Poe would say that it was her Tell

Tale Heart."

11
THE BANKER

J. Farnsworth Kelley turned off the lights in his office and set the alarm before he left the building. As usual, he was the last to leave. He thought it important that the President set a good example for the other bank employees—an example that said, "hard work, long hours, and diligent effort will be rewarded." He was a perfect demonstration of this.

Kelley's black Cadillac sat in its special covered parking space next to the bank's side door. There was not another car in the town of Colbert like it. He'd had to special order the car in Nashville since there was no Cadillac dealership in town. Kelley wanted everyone to know when he drove by—to know that they were close to a man of stature. In fact, everything about him—his car, his name, his house, his clothing, his bearing—was calculated to show the people of this little town just who he was and, by inference, just who they were.

As he drove by the Riverside Shopping Center, his thoughts carried him back forty years. There was no shopping center then. The area was a slum along Willow Creek called "Crawfish Bottoms." When the creek flooded, as it did on a regular basis, the poor residents either camped out on the rocky ridge west of the creek or moved their meager possessions to the upper stories and stayed with them until the water subsided.

Kelley hated it when his thoughts took him back to those days. Although he'd resolved not to think on those times, his mind had no regard for his wishes. Some sight or sound or person would trigger a forgotten key and those forbidden memories would come flooding back. Today the vision was especially acute—*he and his mother racing against the rising water, sometimes in the middle of the night, to get their possessions up the narrow stairs. They had been careful to see that everything in the house could be lifted by the two of them and fitted through the narrow opening to the upstairs room. And the cleaning out of the mud, the crawfish, and sometimes a snake or two after the water left. The severity of the flood just departed was always measured against the highest water mark on the wall in the front room, 26 ¾ inches from the floor*. Yes, he hated it when his mind forced him to revisit these times. Hated it because he felt as if everyone else was viewing the same scenes and knowing—yes, really knowing—who he was.

In those days there was no J. Farnsworth Kelley. His mother called him Jack. To everyone else in town, he was "Crawfish," the little kid from Crawfish Bottoms who pulled the homemade cart through the more affluent sections of town delivering the washing his mother took in. Unable to face the responsibilities of parenthood, his father had left for parts unknown before he was born.

Jack had hated every minute of it. Hated the jeers of the other kids when they pointed out one of their hand-me-down jackets his mother had gotten for him from the "clothes closet" at the Methodist Church. Hated the condescending attitudes of the adults when he picked up and delivered their laundry. Hated it so much that he'd vowed to himself that he'd get even someday, that they would all pay for their snide remarks and slights. He didn't know how he'd do it, but he knew he would. It was that burning in his gut that kept him going.

Today, there were no more Crawfish Bottoms. The town, with Federal help, had razed the slum houses, put Willow Creek in a large metal tunnel, and put up a levee and flood gate where the creek flowed into river. They built brick duplexes for the displaced poor in another section of town. His mother had been so proud of her new home. In a way Jack was glad she had died before it became what it was today—a brick slum that didn't flood.

Just as Crawfish Bottoms had disappeared, so had Jack "Crawfish" Kelley. He was smart and had studied hard in school hoping that good grades would open some doors. They did, but not enough. College was out of the question. So he signed up for a four-year stint in the Navy. It was a calculated move. He placed high on tests and got to choose some excellent training schools. He also got to see quite a bit of the world. But, most importantly, he got money for college. With it, some small student loans, and part-time jobs he got his degree and ranked very high in his class in the process.

It was during college that he changed his name. He had no middle name and "Jack" seemed so common. So he kept the "J" in front and added "Farnsworth" because he thought it sounded important—sounded as if the person bearing it were somebody.

It was also during college that his department head helped him get on part-time at one of the banks where he attracted the attention of one of the executives. That gave him an inside track to a full-time position upon graduation. With ability, hard work, and a strong mentor, he rose rapidly. He was head of one of the bank's branches when he learned that the parent company was buying the leading bank in Colbert. He lobbied hard, and successfully, to be named as its president. He'd left town as Crawfish Kelley in a tight sailor suit; he'd come back as J. Farnsworth Kelley in a three-piece suit and a black Cadillac. Fate had dealt him the hand he'd wished for. It was his to play and play it he had for the last five years.

The little boy pulling the laundry cart thought mostly of getting even in physical terms. The bank president in the Cadillac sought vengeance on the spirit. His bank was the dominant one in town and had most of the loans, mortgages, and financial transactions of any consequence. Kelley loved it when one of his former tormentors or one of his mother's former customers had to come in for a loan or an extension of payment or to seek some financial favor. It was not that he turned them down. On the contrary, most were approved because Kelley prided himself on making good business decisions. However, the petitioner always left knowing who held his financial fate in his hands, who could ruin him if he chose, and who, in a capricious moment, might just choose to do so. Within a year or so of his return, Kelley had most of the leading citizens of the town on edge. He could see it in their eyes and hear it in their voices as he met them at various town functions. Yes, the proverbial chicken had come home to roost.

Kelley's mind came back to the present when he crossed the river and saw the big house at the top of the ridge. It was visible for miles and seemed to dominate the valley and the town. Yes, that house was a long way from Crawfish Bottoms Kelley thought as he turned into its long drive.

After putting the car into the garage, Kelley strolled around the well-kept yard enjoying the view. His wife was in Nashville where she still did a lot of volunteer work. Their only son was away at boarding school. He felt like a Medieval baron as he looked down on the valley and town. Yes, revenge was sweet. He could almost taste it. He savored it and feelings of fruition and contentment flowed through him not unlike the Willow Creek of old at flood tide. Life was, indeed, good.

Kelley strolled around the house to the back yard and was startled out of his mental contentment by the four cows that had thrust their heads through the barbed wire fence and were busily stripping the leaves off his shrubbery. He ran them away and then stood leaning on one of the fence posts thinking.

When the property lines had been set years ago, the crest of the ridge was a natural stopping place for the farms on both sides of it. Kelley had bought one of these small farms and done away with the old house site by the road. He didn't have to build so close to the back property line but the only place for <u>his</u> house was at the top of the hill. This put one of the rear corners of his house only about forty feet from the back pasture fence of the opposite farm. It was owned by an older couple, Zebulum and Boonie Mae Snavely.

When Kelley had selected his house site, he had foreseen no problem with it. But he had not taken the closeness of the Snavely's pasture into consideration. This was not the first time his shrubbery had been eaten. As he leaned on the post and watched the cows graze, the solution came to him. He'd just buy a few acres of the back part of their place and create a buffer zone between his yard and the pasture. Yes, that's what he'd do. He'd tend to this tomorrow.

The next day Kelley did some checking. He never took a step without preparation—without doing his homework. There was no mortgage on the Snavely place and they had no outstanding loans anywhere. Since he would have no leverage, Kelley would have to be at his persuasive best.

When he left the bank that afternoon, he drove on past his place and followed the road around the end of the ridge and up the next valley to the Snavely place. Kelley did not know them well but he knew they had no heirs. He'd gone to school with their only son who had been killed in Vietnam. He and Ronnie had not been friends but he remembered that Ronnie had never teased or made fun of him. When the others did, he just seemed to pull off to one side and not join in.

As Kelley stopped his car in the drive of the Snavely's modest farmhouse, he saw Zebulum coming from the barn and his evening chores. He came around the house to greet his visitor. Boonie Mae came out on the front porch drying her hands on her apron. After the initial greetings, they invited Kelley to sit with them under the large maple tree that dominated the front yard. The vintage chairs were metal with about twenty coats of paint but comfortable. Kelley could see that his reputation had preceded him—that the Snavelys were cautious and apprehensive wondering what he wanted with them.

After a few minutes of small talk about the lack of rain and falling beef prices, Kelley got to the point of his visit. "Mr. Snavely, you know the back of my house and your back pasture fence are right close together. I'd like a little more space behind me so I'd like to buy five acres across the back of your pasture. And just to make sure I treat you right,

I'm prepared to pay you the going rate for good creek bottom farmland for it."

Zebulum heard Kelley's proposal without showing any outward emotion. He glanced at his wife who dropped her eyes, deferring the decision to him. He rocked in his chair, rubbed his chin with its stubble of white beard, and looked up into the branches of the maple, thinking.

Kelley broke in, "Mr. Snavely, I'd be pleased if you'd like to think about this for a few days."

After a few minutes, Zebulum leaned forward in his chair and looked Kelley in the eye. "Tain't no need of doing that. Ah kin give ya' ma' answer rat now. Ah jest don't know as how ah'd wanna sell part of ma' place. Iffen ah ever does sell, hit' ud be better ta' have eighty acres than seventy-five."

Kelley was prepared for just such a turn. "Well then, Mr. Snavely, let me make you an offer for the whole eighty acres." He paused for effect. "Bottom land price for every acre, of course."

"That's a mighty good offer, Mr. Kelley."

"I'm glad you recognize that, Mr. Snavely. I don't think you'll ever get a better one. Here's what it would come to." Kelley handed him a memo pad sheet with the figures on it. Why don't you just consider it for a few days?"

"Naw. Ain't no need ta' do that. Ah jest ain't innerested in sellin' rat now."

Kelley tried to hide his annoyance. "Well now, Mr. Snavely, you know you and the missus aren't getting any younger. This would give you all a nice little nest egg for your later years. You seem like a good business man to me and surely you can see that you're not likely to get a better offer."

"Ah spec you rat, but when a man ain't ready ta' sell, he just ain't ready ta' sell."

There was nothing more to be said but as Kelley rose to go, he could not resist one last parting shot. "You should mark this down, Mr. Snavely. Times may not again be so favorable and the next offer you get might not be so good." Zebulum and Boonie Mae did not miss the veiled threat.

Kelley bided his time waiting for a fortuitous moment. Zebulum's cows continued to eat the shrubs.

Then, one day on his drive home with the car radio set on the local station, he heard the news. A local farmer had gotten careless while mowing on a steep slope. The tractor turned over on him. He was dead when his wife found him. It was Zebulum Snavely. Events had played into Kelley's hands.

After waiting a few weeks—what most would consider a "proper" amount of time—Kelley drove around to the other side of the ridge one afternoon to see Boonie Mae Snavely. She came out as he got out of his car and invited him to sit again under the maple tree.

This time there was no small talk. As Boonie Mae Snavely plopped down in the lime green metal chair she got straight to the point. "Ah guess you's come about the land. Well, iffen ah sells it, ah'm gonna sell the whole thang. Ah ain't innerested in a whole buncha parts." Kelley noted that she seemed much more assertive than she had been on his earlier visit.

"That's fine," replied Kelley as he handed her a slip of paper. "Here's my offer for the whole eighty acres."

Boonie Mae took the paper and stared at it for several minutes. A dark cloud seemed to come across her face. The muscles in her jaw tightened causing noticeable bulges beneath each ear. Finally, she spoke. "Mr. Kelley, this is a lot less than ya' offered me an' Zeb jest a few months ago."

"Yes…yes, you're right, Mrs. Snavely. But you know that land is selling pretty slow right now and land prices are going down." What Boonie Mae didn't know was that Kelley had put out the word that he wanted the Snavely place and that no one else dared make an offer before he either bought it or withdrew. "And," Kelley continued, "I made you and your husband a good offer and you will remember I warned you both that the situation might not continue to be so favorable."

Boonie Mae remembered—she remembered a lot of things. She looked Kelley in the eye but her lower lip trembled as she spoke. "Mr. Kelley, why are ya' doin' this ta' me? Ah know where ya' come from. Ronnie told us how the other kids treated ya'. We always told him not ta' join in. Did he treat ya' bad an' we not know of it? Is this ya' way at gittin' back after all these years?" There was a pleading in her voice as she searched for an answer.

Boonie Mae's questions touched a nerve somewhere deep inside Kelley's being. Perhaps it was a twinge of conscience that he had thought long dead. Kelley pushed it aside. He would not be deterred with his goal so close. "No, Mrs. Snavely, Ronnie was never mean to me. This is just business."

Boonie Mae looked down at the paper that she was turning over and over in her fingers. "Ah'll have ta' think on it, Mr. Kelley."

"Of course, you will. I'll be waiting for your answer," replied Kelley as he made his departure. As he backed down the drive, Boonie Mae was still sitting in the green chair looking at the paper fluttering in her hands.

Kelley didn't expect a quick answer. He thought he'd wait a week or two before he brought any more pressure to bear. It would give her time to realize that she couldn't run the place by herself and that she wasn't going to get any other offers. But within a day or two, Kelley noticed something odd. Boonie Mae was in town every day driving their old beat up pickup and talking to a lot of different people. "Just what could this old woman be up to?" Kelley asked himself. He was soon to find out.

A day or so later and just after getting home for the evening, Kelley thought he heard voices coming from his back yard. Going out to investigate, he found Boonie Mae Snavely and some fellow with an armload of stakes obviously marking off an area in her pasture. She had a long tape measure and some papers on a clipboard. "Naw, not there. Move 'at last 'un two foot up the hill," shouted Boonie Mae as she referred to her clipboard. "Now let's check the width again." The two began dragging the tape around. Kelley walked out to the fence and leaned on a post.

It wasn't long before Boonie Mae noticed him. "Well, hello, Mr. Kelley," she shouted to him as she made her way in his direction. "Ah bin need'un ta' come by an' see ya' but ah jest bin sa' busy." Kelley noted that she seemed excited over something.

"Just what are you laying off over there, Mrs. Snavely?" he asked.

"Mr. Kelley, ah've decided ta' keep ma' place an' go inta' the chicken bizness. You know the chicken plant in town will provide an' deliver the baby chicks an' all the feed an' pick 'um up when they get frying size an' pay ya' fer 'em."

"Chickens?!" Kelley almost shouted incredulously as his mouth dropped open.

"Yes siree," continued Boonie Mae, "an' all ah've gotta have is the chicken house. An' they give ya' plans ta' build it by. This here's gonna be ma' first 'un an' ah've got plenty room fer more iffen this'un works out. Ya' don't want 'um too close ta' yer house on account of the smell."

"But…but…but," Kelley stammered as he looked at the rectangle of stakes only about thirty feet across the fence, "what about <u>my</u> house?"

Boonie Mae looked up as if seeing Kelley's house for the first time. "Well, Mr. Kelley, all ah kin say is ah'll take care of my house, hit's up ta' ya' to take care of yourn. An', as ya' said, this is jest bizness." Boonie Mae turned on her heel and went back to directing the man with the stakes. Kelley stood clinging to the fence post for support.

After a sleepless night, Kelley concluded that Boonie Mae had to be bluffing. He'd just do some checking the next day. He'd find out what she'd been doing in town every day.

Kelley began his search early the next morning. He put out the word and answers were not long in coming. Boonie Mae had met with the president of one of the small banks. It had to be for a loan to build the chicken house but the president would not divulge further information. She'd had at least three meetings with the folks at the chicken plant and had picked up plans and specifications. She had met with two contractors about making bids and had been to the ready-mix concrete plant, the lumberyard, the electrical supply house and the farm supply store. Also, she had been to the county departments checking on building permits and restrictions. The strangest of her activities had been the two meetings with the head of the new investment company. "What did this woman have to invest?" wondered Kelley. But, considering everything, Boonie Mae seemed to be serious. She was doing all the right things. Kelley had to admit that his worst fears were being realized.

For the next several days, Kelley walked out to the fence every day and looked at the stakes. He could almost smell the chickens. Finally, he climbed the fence and walked out among the stakes. From this vantage point, he saw for the first time the double line of stakes that ran over to the fence row and down the hill before crossing the small creek and continuing to the front pasture gate. That had to be the access road. That settled it. Kelley got into his car and drove around to Boonie Mae's.

She did not come out when he drove up. He knocked at the front door and heard sounds of movement inside. Boonie Mae came to the door and invited him in. She ushered him into the living room and asked him to have a seat. The door leading to the dining room was open. Through it Kelley could see the dining table cluttered with blue prints and other papers. At one end a cup of coffee sat where a chair was pulled back. Bonnie Mae was obviously busy working on her project.

"I've come to make another offer," began Kelley.

Boonie Mae cut him off. "At's gud. But afore ya' do, let me make ya' one." She rose from her chair, went into the dining room, picked up a piece of paper from the table, returned, and handed it to Kelley.

He looked at it twice and then looked away blinking his eyes to make sure they were focused. A third look at the paper confirmed his initial reading. The numbers were the same. Kelley was visibly shaken. "Well, Mrs. Snavely, this is a much higher figure than I first offered you and Mr. Snavely. The best land around here's not selling for this price. And furthermore…"

"Ah know, Mr. Kelley," replied Boonie Mae, cutting him off, "but hit seems ta' me that thangs is worth about what somebody's willin' ta' pay. Ma' finance man tells me that with that amount, ah kin get me a little place in town an' with gud investment management, have enough ta' live on 'til ah die."

"Why, this is highway robbery," sputtered Kelley.

"Ah guess ya' could say that, Mr. Kelley. But ah ain't holdin' no gun on ya'. An' ah ain't got but two choices—git this much money or raise chickens. Hit's yore choice what ah do."

Kelley's first impulse was to get emotional—to become indignant about the unfair price or to play on her sympathy. He resisted the urge. His years in business had taught him better. In a situation like this, it was best just to take your losses and go on. Boonie Mae held all the cards and Kelley had nothing left in the hole. Both knew exactly where the other stood. Boonie Mae sat patiently waiting for Kelley's response.

"I'll need to think about this for a few days." Kelley was grasping at the straws of time, hoping that he could come up with something—anything—that would alter the situation.

"Well, Mr. Kelley, ya'd better think fast. This is Thursday an' the contractor is comin' Monday ta' start the road."

Kelley's shoulders slumped. If he let her get the road started, the price would probably go up. "Be at my office at ten in the morning and I'll draw up the papers."

"Kin ah bring ma' finance man with me ta' look over them papers?" she asked.

Boonie Mae was leaving nothing to chance. "Bring anyone you want," answered Kelley as he rose from his chair. "I'll see myself out."

"Boonie Mae! Boonie Mae! Air you in thar?" Sioda Fitzhugh yelled through the front screen door.

Boonie Mae yelled back, "Come on back ta' the kitchen, Sioda!" The two women had no problem recognizing the other's voice. They had lived across the road from each other for over fifty years.

Sioda pushed her way through the boxes strewn about the house leaning heavily on her walking stick. Boonie Mae was wrapping and packing dishes. She looked up as Sioda struggled through the kitchen door. "What in the name of Pete are ya' doin' with that cane, Sioda?"

"Ah ain't had a gud week," reported Sioda as she

dropped heavily into a chair. "Ah wuz cleanin' out that thicket behind the house tother day an' ah creeled my ankle a rat smart."

"Ya' hadn't oughta be doing stuff like that," scolded Boonie Mae.

"Ah know that. But with my Clyde being dead goin' on nine year now, ah've found out that a woman's gotta do what a woman's gotta do." That had become Sioda's favorite statement since her husband's death. It was meant to evoke sympathy as well as to show her resolve to go on with life. Boonie Mae had heard it a thousand times. "An' that's not the half of it, Boonie Mae. Last Monday night a limb fell offen that big beech down below the barn an' broke down a section of fence an ma' milk cow got out. Hit wuz nigh on to noon afore ah found her eatin' vines over by the Johnson place. Ah gotta rope an' tied her to the back of the car an' drove home with her. But ah had ta' drive so slow that the car overheated an' boiled all the water otta the radiator. Ah didn't think ah'd ever git that thang cooled off. But you know what ah always say. A woman's gotta do..."

"Yes, Sioda, ah know," interrupted Boonie Mae. She didn't feel the need to hear the statement again.

"Looks like yer gittin' packed up pretty gud."

"Yes, hit's comin' rat along."

"Ah'm shore gonna miss ya' 'round here. Ah guess Mr. Kelley done give ya' a gud price for ya' place though."

Boonie Mae recognized the hint but she was not about to reveal what she'd been paid. "Yes, hit were gud enough."

"But ah fer one am shore disappointed fer ya'," Sioda

continued, "that ya' didn't get ta' live out ya' dream."

"What dream ya' talkin' 'bout?"

"Why yore dream of coverin' that hillside with chicken houses an' bein' somebody in the bizness world an' makin' lotsa money an"...

Boonie Mae cut her off short. "That weren't never my dream. Ah hate chickens. Ah couldn't stand the few we had ta' have 'bout the place. Always nestin' in the wrong places, peckin' yore fingers, leavin' their droppin's all over the front porch, scratchin' up yer flowers. Ah never could stand the nasty things."

"But...But...But..." Sioda stammered, "what 'bout all the work an' plannin' ya' done, the blue prints, stakin' off the place, all the meetin's ya' had, an' ya' told everybody what ya' wuz a gonna do?"

"You should know the answer ta' that better'un anybody," Boonie Mae answered.

"Ah should?"

"Yes, ya' should, Sioda." Boonie Mae wrapped the last cup and put it into the box before looking over her glasses at her neighbor. "As ya' always say, a woman's gotta do what a woman's gotta do."

12
ALWAYS IN CHARACTER

There were cars and trucks, mostly trucks, in the parking lot and the front porch lights were on at the Braceyville Funeral Home, a sure sign that some local resident was laid out in the front room with the lid open. Like moths attracted to a streetlight, the townspeople were drawn to the funeral home's brightly-lit porch. Whether they knew the deceased well or not, it was a good time to visit as well as to pay last respects. Most everybody in town could be counted on to drop by sometime during the evening.

On this particular evening, the honoree was Tub Pickett. He lay in a cheap coffin surrounded by two or three scraggly flower arrangements. Tub would not be much missed.

Most folks supposed that Tub got his name because of his extra large beer gut. It was the largest any of the local residents could remember seeing. It drooped somewhere near mid-thigh and was about the size of a wash tub. But Tub got his name when he was a mere infant and before he had ever tasted beer. He had an older brother who was assigned the chore of watching out for him when his parents were both away from home. This brother loved to hunt and fish, so as soon as his parents were out of sight, he would put the infant under a number three wash tub somewhere in the yard and head for the woods or the creek. One day the Picketts came home early forcing the older boy to stop this practice. The tub was gone but the name remained.

The visitors spilled out onto the front porch and into the front lawn. Few cared much about Tub Pickett; they were here to see Miss Jenny May Shannon. There was an air of expectancy. Those who came late would ask, "Miss Jenny been in yet?" and there were other comments:

"I bet she ain't comin'."

"I bet she does."

"Would you come iffen you wuz her?"

"Nope. But I ain't her and she ain't missed comin' in more'n fifty year."

"There's always a first time."

"Not fer Miss Jenny they ain't."

Miss Jenny May Shannon had taught English and directed plays at the high school in the little coal company town until she was nearly eighty. The consolidation of grades nine through twelve into Lake City and the fact that she had no way to get there had forced her into retirement. She had taught everyone in town who had gone through Braceyville High. Tub Pickett had not been one of her students. If he had been, things might have turned out differently.

Miss Jenny always came to the funeral home with words of comfort for the grieving family and always with something nice to say about the deceased. It was one of Braceyville's traditions. Most people wouldn't think it was a proper burial unless Miss Jenny said some complimentary words about the dear departed and shed a tear or two. But then, none of the others had been Tub Pickett.

Tub had not been one of the town's more exemplary citizens. He had worked as a miner for the Bracey Coal Company, the largest coal company in that area of Appalachia. His days had been spent in the mine. His nights—until closing time—had been spent at Darryl's

Tavern drinking beer. It was Tub's nighttime activity that had gotten the whole controversy started. One evening he was headed home after several hours of beer consumption. He had parked his truck in front of Miss Jenny's house, a few doors down from the tavern. When he got to his vehicle, he realized that he had not emptied out the last gallon or so of beer. There was a large geranium bush in the corner of Miss Jenny's front yard by the sidewalk which exactly fitted Tub's need at that moment. So, he proceeded to relieve himself in the bush before driving off.

This initial act seemed to awaken some perverted instinct deep inside Tub. On future nights when he parked down toward Miss Jenny's, he would make it a point to give her geranium a good spraying on his way home. Pretty soon he began to park in front of Miss Jenny's every night on purpose just so he could pee on her bush.

This nightly dose of urine was not good for the bush's health. It soon began to wither and die on the street side. Miss Jenny noticed its condition but was at a loss as to why just part of an otherwise healthy geranium would die. She thought it might have something to do with the terrible smell that was so prominent on that side but she could not figure out the source of the odor either.

Then, one night the truth came out. Miss Jenny usually retired early but this particular night her cat had not come back in. She was out in the yard looking for him when Tub Pickett came reeling down the sidewalk. Not wanting anyone to see her in her nightgown, she stepped behind a large maple tree to await his departure. Her eyes widened in horror as she observed Tub performing his nightly ritual. Forgetting her state of dress for the moment, she rushed out of her hiding place waving her cane and shouting in a high-pitched voice. "You stop that, Tub Pickett! You sorry no-good! You've been peeing on my bush and killing it. Now stop messing up my yard and get out of here!"

Miss Jenny's verbal attack hardly fazed Tub. He continued until his bladder was empty and then staggered to his truck, laughing at her.

From that point on, Tub became more sadistic. He would shout insults and cuss at her each night as he wet down the geranium. This disruption of her sleep began to tell on Miss Jenny. She went to the town constable but he was afraid of Tub and said that he couldn't do anything unless he caught him in the act. Of course, he never could seem to get around at the right time. Soon the whole of Braceyville knew what was going on. The bush continued to die.

Then one night Rick Stagg, who had been working late at the coal company office, stopped by Darryl's for a beer on his way home. He had been one of Miss Jenny's best students and had been the lead actor in several of her plays. He worked in the coal company's office keeping records.

Tub Pickett was in his usual place. Because he knew Rick was interested in such things, Tub began talking to him about the new CB radio he'd just bought for his truck. Since it was near closing time, he invited Rick to come down to his truck and see it.

As the two got to where the truck was parked, Tub veered off course toward the geranium bush unzipping his fly. "Wait jest a minute while I tend to this first."

"Don't do that, Tub." There was an edge on Rick's voice.

"And jest why not?" Tub asked sarcastically.

"Cause Miss Jenny's a nice lady and she's old and there's just no sense in making her last years miserable and peeing on her bush."

Rick's words sent Tub into a frenzy. "You little pencil pusher! Jest cause you work in the office you think you're better'n me and can tell me what to do! Les' see how you'd like a good dose of ol' Bessie!"

Tub lurched to his truck and grabbed the shotgun from the gun rack. When he turned around, he was looking down the barrel of Rick's forty-five automatic. Since he had to carry money and important papers for the coal company, they had gotten him a permit and insisted that he carry a gun.

The pistol and the look in Rick's face brought Tub to a momentary halt. But it only lasted a few seconds. "Why you little shit. You ain't got guts enough to use that thang." With that he started to pump a shell into the gun's chamber. He never finished. The forty-five made two large holes in the middle of Tub's chest and drove him back against the truck's side and down onto the asphalt street.

It was getting close to eight o'clock and no sign of Miss Jenny. Suddenly, her porch light came on, her front door opened, and Miss Jenny May Shannon, dressed in her black mourning clothes, stepped out. As she made her way along the sidewalk, a hush fell on those in the funeral home's front yard and gradually extended to those on the porch and then to those inside. The only sounds were an occasional throat clearing and the tap, tap, tap of Miss Jenny's cane. The crowd parted for her as the waters had for Moses as she made her way across the porch. She went on inside and sat down with two ladies, Mrs. Whitney and Mrs. Helton, sisters with whom she had taught for many years.

The three made polite small talk for a few minutes. The murmur of other voices began to increase in volume but no one's eyes left Miss Jenny for very long. All wondered what she'd say about Tub Pickett, the man who had peed on her geranium nightly and who'd gotten himself killed in front of her house for doing it.

Finally, Miss Jenny heaved a big sigh. "I guess it's time to give Tub a last look," she said as she got to her feet. The room fell silent. She walked toward the open casket with Mrs. Helton on one side and Mrs. Whitney on the other. Each put an arm around her as if to give support and comfort. Miss Jenny really needed neither of these. The two women intended to make sure they heard what Miss Jenny had to say.

They stood before the open lid for several minutes. Tub looked better in death than he ever had in life. At length Miss Jenny broke the silence, "Well, I'll have to give him credit for one thing."

There was a long pause. The sisters looked at each other. "What's that, Miss Jenny?" asked Mrs. Whitney.

Drawing on her many years' experience in directing drama, Miss Jenny replied, "He always stayed in character."

Miss Jenny turned to go. It was obvious she intended to say no more. There were more quizzical looks between the sisters. Mrs. Helton felt that it was her turn to ask for clarification, so she put her hand on Miss Jenny's arm to delay her departure. "In character, Miss Jenny?"

‘Yes, in character,” answered Miss Jenny. “He was an ass-hole to the very end.”

13
THE SPIRIT OF ELVIS

The day began like any other normal Tuesday. There was no indication of the impending disaster. Inez donned her Elvis jacket and walking shoes and set out on her morning trek around the neighborhood. Bill got into his car and headed for the City Café and the meeting of the Community Coffee Club where all problems from the local to the international level were analyzed and solved. Bill didn't drink coffee; Dr. Pepper was his liquid of choice. Nothing lifted his spirits each day more than a cold Dr. Pepper over ice and one of Burnell's fried pies--peach, apple, or apricot—with two scoops of vanilla bean ice cream. Peach was Bill's favorite. Thoughts of the approaching treat caused his mouth to begin to water like a Pavlovian dog as he turned onto Main Street.

Inez's walk was mostly uneventful. She exchanged greetings with a few of her neighbors who were working in their yards. Then, about a block from her house, disaster struck. She came upon the rear end of a large, brown mule standing next to the street and grazing in Beulah Pollard's flowers. The sight startled her and her abrupt halt caused her shoes to make a scraping noise in the grit on the sidewalk. The mule swung around to locate the sound and stared straight at Inez with a purple petunia dangling from the corner of his mouth. She hardly knew what to do. She'd never had a face-off with a mule before but she didn't feel as if she were in any danger. The mule seemed docile and non-aggressive. He just stood blocking her path, staring at her, and munching on a mouthful of flowers.

After a minute or two, Inez decided on a course of action. She would give the mule a wide berth, go on home, and call somebody to come and deal with the situation. She walked out in the street and back onto the sidewalk while watching the mule out of the corner of her eye. Only his head moved as his eyes followed her path. She gave a sigh of relief as she regained the sidewalk and began to move away. But then she heard the "clop, clop, clop." A glance back over her shoulder confirmed that the mule was following her. She increased her pace. The mule increased his. She began to trot. So did the mule. Knowing she could not outrun him, she slowed to a normal pace. The mule matched his pace to hers. Inez could feel his hot breath on her neck and every few steps he would push her in the small of the back with his nose causing her to stumble. The metallic taste of fear filled her mouth. What if he pushed her down and trampled her to death? She was thankful her house was close.

Normally, she went in through the kitchen but the front door was closer. As she turned up the walk, she got her keys out of her pocket and found the one she needed. Halfway up the walk the mule poked her in the back with his nose and then clamped his teeth down on the loose fabric near the top of her left sleeve. Inez almost panicked. She tried to jerk her jacket out of the mule's mouth but his teeth held like a vise. Surely he wouldn't follow her into the house. But he did march up the three steps to the porch and push on inside the living room when she opened the door. Inez was beside herself. As the two crossed the room with her still trying to snatch her jacket from captivity, the mule's head hit the overhead light fixture startling him into releasing his grip. While he was distracted by the light's swinging, Inez escaped into the hall and slammed the door shut behind her.

Exhausted, she fell into a chair and tried to recover while listening to the mule's clomping about her living room. After her heart slowed to an almost normal rate, she removed her jacket to assess the damage. It was one of her prize possessions. She had purchased it several years earlier on a trip to Graceland. It was white satin with a full-length Elvis on the back dressed in a gold, lame jump suit playing a guitar. Black musical notes sprang from the instrument and swirled around the smiling figure and over the right shoulder to the jacket's front. On the upper left chest were the words "The King."

There were several blobs of mule slobber on Elvis and a few bits of chewed flower leaves on the part that had been in the mule's mouth. But there didn't seem to be any tears or permanent damage. Inez breathed a sigh of relief.

Several minutes passed with no sounds coming from the living room. Maybe the mule had gone back outside. Inez knew she'd left the front door open. She hung the jacket on the back of the chair, tiptoed to the hall door, opened it just a crack, and peeked inside. Her heart sank when she saw that the mule was still in residence. He had backed into the front corner between the end of the couch and a gold, wing back chair. He moved his ears as he gazed at the still swaying light fixture. Inez shut the door and tried to think what to do next.

She had to get that mule out of the house before Bill got home. He was always accusing her of doing wacky things—because, basically, she was always doing wacky things. But this one topped all the others put together. He'd never let her live it down.

She tried to think rationally. The mule hadn't tried to hurt her. He seemed nice and even-tempered. Maybe she could lure him back outside. She thought of the sack of ears of yellow corn Bill kept in the garage for squirrel food. They looked so cute sitting up on that little bench with their tails up while they ate. She put five or six ears into a plastic dishpan and slipped back into the living room. The mule had not done too much damage. The coffee table was turned over with the things it held scattered over the carpet. He had knocked three or four pictures off the wall backing into the corner. The worst thing was the dirty hoof marks on and a couple of tears in her new carpet.

The mule just looked at her. The light fixture had stopped swinging. He did not offer to move. Inez took a deep breath, walked over to him, set the corn on the floor in front of him, and backed up a couple of steps. The mule dropped his nose, muzzled the ears, and selected one. He bit it in two and began to chew up the portion remaining in his mouth cob and all. In the process pieces of corn, cob, and slobber fell out of his mouth and mostly on the carpet. Inez wanted to cry at the mess being made but she bit her lip and resolved to see her plan through. She stepped forward and dragged the dishpan away three or four feet. Her hopes were to lure him a few feet with each bite and gradually get him through the front door. However, after finishing his first mouthful, the mule stepped forward with one foot, dropped his nose into the dishpan, and dragged it back to its original position. He bit another ear in two and stood watching Inez as he chewed. It was a Mexican standoff. Inez went back to the kitchen and dialed the police department.

The taste of fried peach pie and ice cream was still in Bill's mouth as he returned home. As he neared his street, he noted a number of cars parked along the main street and thought that Tuesday was an odd day for a yard sale. Then he saw the blue lights flashing on the patrol car blocking the entrance to his street and Patrolman Ernie Satterfield directing traffic to go on by. Ernie had been one of Bill's students. In fact everybody under fifty in town had been one of Bill's students at some point. Ignoring Ernie's frantic waving, Bill nosed his car up to the patrol car and rolled down his window. Ernie came around to the driver's side hitching up his gun belt until he saw who it was. "Oh, hi, Mr. Bill," he said as he touched the visor of his cap.

"What the hell's going on, Ernie?"

"Well, sir, we've got a little problem."

"Problem? What kind of problem? Where is it?"

"Well, sir, it's down at your house."

"What is it?"

"Well, sir, a mule has gotten inside your house."

Bill's mouth dropped open and it was several seconds before he could exclaim," A WHAT?"

"Yes, sir, a mule. I know it sounds funny but that's what we've got."

"Good lord!" said Bill, the look of disbelief still on his face. "Ernie, move your car so I can get down there and see about it."

"I'm sorry, sir, but the chief told me not to let anybody down this street."

"For crying out loud, Ernie, I'm not just anybody! It's my house! I'm involved! Get that damn car out of the way!"

The old principal-student relationship surfaced as Ernie scrambled to do Bill's biding saying, "Yes, sir. Yes, sir."

As Bill drove toward his house, he could see the blue lights of the patrol car blocking the other end of his street. However, it was obvious these measures were not going to deter a crowd from gathering. Curiosity seekers were parking on other streets and coming through peoples' yards to get to the scene. "How in the world did Inez manage this?" he thought to himself. "I've always cautioned her about letting strangers in while I'm gone. I guess I'm going to have to include animals as well."

Pulling into his driveway, Bill noted the open front door and Lester Hatfield, the town's Chief of Police, stringing around his front yard yellow tape with the words, "Police Crime scene—Do Not Cross," printed on it. Lester was also one of Bill's former students. Inez did not see Bill immediately. She was under a maple tree on the other side of the yard being interviewed by Jock Sullivan, a cub reporter from the Grove City Gazette. Jock was not a native.

Bill ducked under the tape and said, "Hey, Lester."

"Why, howdy, Mr. Bill, replied the Chief looking up from his task with the tape.

"Please tell me what Ernie just told me's not so."

"I'm afraid it is, Mr. Bill—and he's a big'un too."

"Where in the hell did he come from?" asked Bill.

"The current ownership of the animal in question has not

been determined at the present time," stated Lester lapsing into cop talk.

Inez spied Bill and came rushing across the yard. She threw her arms around him exclaiming, "Oh, Bill, I'm so glad you're back!"

After a few seconds, Bill managed to extricate himself from her grasp and ask, "How in the name of Pete did this happen?"

Before Inez could respond, Bill felt a tugging on his arm and turned to see Jock with his pen poised over his note pad; another pen was behind his ear; his hat had the front brim turned up to the crown with his press card sticking in the band. He looked like something out of the forties. "Sir, he asked, "could you tell me your reaction to returning home to find a mule occupying your living room?"

Chief Lester took over at this point. "Son, get your butt behind that tape!"

"Sir, I am a reporter. Have you never heard of freedom of the press?"

"I'll tell you what you're gonna hear pretty quick and that's your ass landing out in the street where I'm gonna kick it if you don't get it behind my tape," Lester retorted angrily.

Jock scurried behind the tape and began to interview the onlookers at random.

Bill turned back to Inez. "He just followed me home," she whined.

"Followed you home? A mule followed you home? No,

Inez. A puppy follows you home. Or you pick up a stray kitten. Mules are not known for following people home."

"But he did," insisted Inez as she went on to relate the events that had brought the mule into their home.

"You say he had a hold of your jacket?" asked Bill.

"That's right."

"Well, why in the devil didn't you just slip out of it and let the mule have it?" asked Bill.

"I did think about that, hon, but I just couldn't let a mule have it. Elvis would never have forgiven me."

"Why in hell would Elvis care? He's been dead for twenty-five years."

"But his spirit lives on."

"Maybe so. But I'll bet his spirit doesn't give a rat's ass about that jacket. We could have bought another one. Better to do that than to let a mule destroy our house."

"Oh, honey, you know we couldn't get another one like that. They don't make that style anymore. You remember we looked last August when we were at Graceland for the candlelight vigil."

Bill turned abruptly. "Well, it's too late to be arguing about the blamed jacket now. I'm going inside and see what he's tearing up."

Bill and Chief Lester entered the living room. "Good lord and Saint Agnes!" exclaimed Bill. He takes up half the room!"

"I told you he was a big'un," said Lester.

The mule just stood flopping his ears back and forth and staring at the two men as he finished the last of the corn. Lester walked up beside the mule's head and patted him on the neck. The mule rubbed his head on Lester's chest and made sort of a purring sound in his throat. "He's real gentle," observed Lester as he put his arm around his neck, made a clucking sound with his mouth, and tried to lead the mule out of the corner. The mule responded by setting his front feet and dropping his haunches against the wall. "But he ain't coming outta that corner."

"Just what do you plan to do?" asked Bill.

"I don't rightly know, Mr. Bill. I was thinking if we could find his owner, maybe he would know what to do. I've had it announced on the local radio station."

"That's probably about as good as you're gonna do right now, I guess," Bill replied.

As the two men walked back outside, they surprised Jock who had slithered through the boxwoods at the end of the porch and was trying to take a picture through the living room window. "You damned idiot!" screamed Lester. "If you don't get away from my crime scene, I'm gonna throw your freedom of the press butt in jail!" Jock made a running dive back through the boxwoods losing one pen and his hat which was left hanging in one of the bushes. He shouted back through the shrubbery, "Chief Hatfield, I want you to know you're thwarting a news story that has the potential to be the story of the decade for this town. Why, it could even start me on the road to a Pulitzer and you're blocking the writing of it." Lester just ignored him.

Before they could get off the porch, they heard a

commotion down at one end of the street. A white pick-up with a flashing amber light on top had driven around the patrol car and through a couple of yards and was headed for the scene. The driver was blowing the horn and had one arm out the window, waving people out of his way. The truck came to a skidding halt in the street in front of Bill's house. It was obviously new. The neat letters on the door proclaimed, "Grove City, Animal Control." The driver jumped out leaving the door open and came hurriedly toward the house. His new, blue coveralls had "Sparky," stitched on the pocket. It was Sparky Pitts, the first director of the newly created Animal Control Department. He ducked under the tape and approached Bill and Lester. "Good morning, Chief, Mr. Bill"—another of Bill's former students.

"Morning, Sparky," greeted Lester. "What brings you out this way?"

"I heard there's an animal problem out here and since I'm the Animal Control Director, I thought I ought to get here and be in charge."

"Well, Sparky, it's not good for you to get to thinking that way," said Lester. His voice was a little testy.

Sparky looked about and not seeing any animals asked, "Where's the problem?"

"It's in the house," answered Lester.

"My gosh, Mr. Bill, have you been invaded by a skunk or maybe a rabid coon?"

"Naw," responded Bill. "None of that. Take a look inside."

Sparky went to the door, stuck his head in, and jumped

back. He rubbed his eyes and looked in again just to make sure of what he thought he saw the first time. "Great gobs of goat crap!" he exclaimed. How'd that big thing get in there?'

"How he got in ain't the problem," retorted Lester. "It's how we're gonna get him out is the problem and I'm sure you in your important role as the Director of Animal Control are just gonna lay out the solution for us." Lester's words dripped with sarcasm.

Sparky stood for a minute with his face screwed up in hard thought., Suddenly, his eyes lit up and he said, "I've got it," and went rushing back to his truck. He returned shortly carrying an odd looking rifle

"What the hell is that?" asked Lester. "We don't want to kill him."

"Oh, this won't kill him," Sparky explained. "This is my new tranquilizer gun. I've been dying to try it out. I'll just shoot him with one of these darts and he'll go to sleep in a few minutes and we can just carry him out."

Lester looked disdainfully at Sparky and then said, "Boy, you must have at least four screws loose in your head. You go shooting a dart in that mule's butt and he's liable to tear half the house down before it takes effect. And if you do get him down, how are you going to carry him out? He must weigh twelve hundred pounds. It'd take a forklift. And how would you carry him through the door lying down? He barely fits through it standing up."

"I never thought of all that," said Sparky obviously dejected.

"I know," said Lester his voice taking on a soothing tone.

"But I think there's a way you can help us." Sparky's face brightened. "Don't you have a bunch of books in your new office that tells how to control animals?"

"Yes, sir. I sure do," admitted Sparky.

Lester put one arm around Sparky's shoulders and began to walk him toward his truck as he talked to him. "Now, here's what I need you to do. We need the word of the experts on this matter. So you go back to your office, get them books down, and see what they say to do in a situation like this. First, I'd look under 'mule' and if you don't find anything, go to 'horse' and then to other animals that have four legs that are similar to mules. Maybe 'zebras.' They're just wild mules with stripes. Then there's 'donkeys' and maybe 'camels' and I'm sure you can think of a lot more you being in the animal control business like you are. And if you don't locate anything under the animals, work from the other direction with 'rooms.' Start with 'living room' because that's where our problem is. But you might find it listed under another room in the house like 'bedroom' or 'dining room' or 'kitchen.' Then again the answer might be just under 'house' or maybe 'brick house' or 'two-story house.' I'm sure you get the picture."

Sparky was nodding enthusiastically. "Yes, sir. I sure do."

"And when you find out what the experts say, you call me right away."

"I sure will Chief," replied Sparky as he jumped into his truck and sped away.

"You handled that real well, Lester," said Bill.

"It didn't take too much," said Lester modestly. "That boy never has been too heavy upstairs." Bill just smiled.

Bill's front yard was beginning to look like a circus. Inez was sitting on the little iron bench being consoled by two of her friends. Onlookers were lined up all around the tape. Jock Sullivan was moving amongst them interviewing any who would talk to him. Most seemed to have some opinion on what should be done. Two enterprising young men had carried in a large cooler of beer and were selling it for three dollars a can.

"Mr. Bill, I don't know what the hell we're gonna do," Lester confided as they walked across the yard.

"Don't feel bad about it," Bill responded. "You didn't cause the mess. I'm just as stumped as you are."

Hearing a commotion behind them, Bill and Lester turned around to see a fellow coming under the tape carrying a halter with a length of rope attached to it. Bill recognized Benny Purcell, another of his former students, who had a big farm south of town but lived about three blocks over. After greeting Bill and Lester, Benny said, "I hear there's a mule over here."

"You heard right," responded Lester. "Is he yours?"

"I sure hope so. I've lost one of my best 'uns. He's part of the team that pulls my fancy wagon every year down in Columbia on Mule Day. His name is Ben."

"He didn't give us his name," replied Lester.

"Well, where is he?" asked Benny as he looked around the yard.

"He's in the living room," answered Lester.

Benny almost dropped the halter. "He's where?'

Lester was about to get tired of this reaction every time he gave out the mule's location to a new arrival. "Oh, hell, Benny, pick up your jaw and come on in and look."

As soon as Benny walked into the room, the mule snorted and bobbed his head in recognition. "Ben, you sorry rascal. What are you doing in Mr. Bill's house?" asked Benny as he began to rub and pat the mule. Ben reciprocated by rubbing his head against his owner who continued talking. "You didn't have to slip you halter and run off. I told you I'd be back just as soon as I got your trailer fixed." Ben seemed to understand.

"Mr. Bill, you got anything to make a ramp out of for those steps?" asked Benny. "They'll walk up steps but you'll play hell getting them to walk down." Bill got a couple of volunteers out of the spectators and had a ramp laid down in just a few minutes. He came back inside. Benny had put Ben's halter on. He began to rub his head and ears and talk to him in a quiet voice "Now, Ben, you've had a nice visit with Mr. Bill but you need to come on home so we can get you back to the farm." As he talked, he began to pull harder on the halter rope. Suddenly, Ben set his front legs and backed into the corner so hard that the whole house shook. "Oh, shit!" exclaimed Benny.

"What's wrong?" asked Lester.

"He's balked," answered Benny.

"And that's bad?" asked Bill.

"You're danged right it's bad. He ain't about to move

unless something or somebody moves him."

"What can you do?" Lester wanted to know.

"Well, if he was out in the open, we'd get a bunch behind to push and three or four in front to pull. But we can't do that here. Sometimes we build a fire under them and when it gets hot enough, they move."

"I'd prefer us not go that route," said Bill.

The three men stood around the living room and looked at the mule and each other. The spectators outside waited with much anticipation. The beer vendors had gone for another load.

Finally, Benny asked, "Just how did he get in here in the first place?"

"Inez is the one to tell you about that," Bill answered. He went to the door and called her inside. "Honey, tell Benny here exactly what happened this morning." She related the chain of events.

Benny stood thinking for a minute or so. "You say he got hold of your jacket with his teeth?"

"That's right."

"Would your jacket happen to be white?"

"Why, it sure would. How'd you know?"

"The fellow that works Ben on the farm wears a white jacket a lot. I think ole Ben was lost out on the street and your jacket was the only familiar thing he saw. Where is it?"

Inez took him back to where it was still hanging on the chair. "That's got to be it," said Benny. "Let's see if he'll follow this thing back outside." The garment was too small for Benny to put on so he just draped it over his shoulders and tied the sleeves around his neck. Inez winced. She hated to see Elvis treated that way.

When Benny reentered the room, Ben became more animated, tossing he head around and snorting. Benny got the halter rope, backed out in front of the mule, and turned his back. "Come on ole boy. Here's that jacket you like." Ben stretched his neck out as far as he could but Benny had positioned himself just out of his reach. The mule pawed the floor in frustration making several more tears in the carpet. Benny continued to talk to him. "Come on now. You've gotta come out here to get it." Ben took a couple of small steps and stretched out his neck again but Benny had moved out of his reach. "Come on, Ben. Get outta that corner and come on outside." The mule took a couple more steps without pawing the floor. Benny moved again still encouraging him. "Come on. I know you can do it." The steps were small but the progress was steady. Just before he got to the door, Benny let the mule catch up. He grabbed a mouthful of Elvis and began to shake the jacket vigorously from side to side. Inez began to sob. Bill grabbed her and rushed her out the hall door. He wasn't about to let anything distract the mule at this point. He left her in a chair, crying and moaning, "Poor Elvis, poor Elvis."

When animal and owner got out on the front porch, Ben lifted his tail and fertilized a large portion of it including two wicker chairs. A gasp went up from the spectators. One man dropped his beer. This task completed, he clomped down the ramp to the sidewalk where he stretched out his rear legs, leaned forward, and peed about four gallons right on the concrete. This time the crowd clapped and cheered which seemed to inspire the mule. He began to prance as Benny walked him around the yard to loosen him up. The shouts and cheers grew louder. Ben responded by kicking up his heels and passing gas in their direction. As if by magic, Jock appeared next to Benny with his pad and pen. "Can you tell me if he did any of that inside?"

"Naw, my mule's house broke," joked Benny.

"That would be a colorful element to add to my story," observed Jock. "Could you tell me how you house break a mule? Do you have to use a lot of newspaper?"

Lester's shouting, "Dang you, Jock!" told the reporter that he'd been discovered so he dived back under the tape.

After things had calmed down and Benny had gotten Ben to release the jacket, Bill and Lester were thanking him for getting the mule out of the house. Benny turned to Bill. "Mr. Bill, I'm sure sorry for the damage Ben did to your house. If you won't press any charges against me or sue me, I'll make it right. Just whatever it costs, you know I'm good for it.

"That's mighty nice of you," Bill responded. "I think that'll be just fine."

"What about pain and suffering?" piped up Jock. He had materialized again.

Lester had his mouth open to yell at him again when he was stopped by Bill's upraised hand. Bill put an arm around Jock's shoulder and walked him over under a hackberry tree. "Son, you're not from around here and I didn't have you in school but you need to understand some things if you intend to live and do well. First of all, you need to understand us local folks and how we settle things. Secondly, if you keep on antagonizing Chief Hatfield, he's gonna give you a new understanding of what pain and suffering really means. Do you get my drift?"

"Yes, sir, I think I do."

"Okay then. Now, you just run on down to your office and get your story written," Bill directed.

"Yes, sir." Jock started away.

"But, one more thing."

"Yes, sir"

"Please try not to make Inez look like a damn fool."

"Yes, sir. I think that can be done" agreed Jock as he headed toward town.

Bill and Inez spent most of the afternoon taking phone calls about the incident and cleaning up the house and yard. Some of their friends came to help them pick up the beer cans and other trash and to wash down the porch and sidewalk. Inez worked some to get her Elvis jacket back in shape.

As they were turning in for the night, Inez said, "I've been thinking about what happened today and I think I know what saved us—what got that mule out of the living room."

"Well, what have you decided?" asked Bill.

"It was the spirit of Elvis. Seems like I could just feel his presence. He got in that jacket and led that mule outside."

"Well, I think there's another thing you ought to

consider."

"What's that?"

Bill rolled over and pulled the covers up under his chin. "It was Elvis who led the blame mule in here to start with."

14
JOURNEY TO MEMPHIS

The hills were behind him now and the interstate was flatter and straighter. No more worry about getting behind the semis pulling a long hill side by side and blocking both lanes. In the back of his mind, he was hoping for slow trucks, or maybe one jack-knifed across both lanes, or a construction stoppage lasting for a couple of hours—anything that would make it impossible for him to make the luncheon meeting. Then he could just drive across the median and head back home. He was tempted to do that anyway but something made him keep the nose of the car pointed down the ribbon of concrete which led to Memphis.

He'd fought off attending this gathering for several years—couldn't go before he retired. But Reed was persistent. Kept calling every year or so. And now, after he'd retired from the University, he couldn't offer a good excuse. Reed meant well. A retired minister, he wanted to get all the old bunch together. They'd had some good teams in those years—the early '50s. But that was over fifty years ago now. That was then. Time to let it go. A bunch of old, overweight jocks reliving their glory days.

The phone call had come unexpectedly. He'd not had time to work up a good excuse. So he'd agreed to come and had filled out and sent back the data sheet Reed had mailed to him. He felt trapped—no good way out now. He sort of hoped he'd get sick but that didn't happen. The car seemed to eat up the highway. A green sign flashed by "Memphis 105" it read.

He didn't know why they wanted him back. He hadn't played. But he would have if it had not been for that wet night in Clarksdale. He'd been one of the top backs in the state—6'3", 195, fast and powerful. Coach Rich, Tech's head coach, was calling him every week, promising a scholarship on signing day. Big Fred, Tech's biggest booster in town came to all the games and most practices and made sure that Tech stayed at the top of his list. Other schools called and sent letters but he had his sights set on Tech. But then, it rained and the footing was not good. He'd thought many times after that night just how much a person's life can be changed by one simple thing—rain or no rain or a few steps one way rather than another or a few seconds earlier or later.

They were driving late in the fourth quarter. The big linebacker met him as he broke through the line. On a dry field, he'd never have touched him but his left foot slipped when he planted it to cut leaving the leg to take the hit. His knee had never hurt so badly. He tried to walk but it wouldn't hold his weight. His season was over.

After it healed he worked hard on rehab—harder than he'd ever worked to get it in shape—and the knee came back, to a point. He could still run as fast but he couldn't cut consistently on that leg. Coach Rich quit calling. His folks had no money for college. His dad suggested he put in an application at the rubber plant. Damn that rain!

But Big Fred had taken a liking to him and had prevailed upon Coach Rich to give him a scholarship to be an equipment manager for the team. It wasn't what he'd wanted but it was what he <u>had</u> to do to go to college. So he did it and did it well even though it wasn't pleasant much of the time. Of course, there were some good times but sorting jock straps and trying to keep the players from stealing the new socks and tee shirts got old pretty quickly. His boss would tell him to do something and he'd do it which would piss off some prima donna who would bitch at him and then go to a coach who would chew him out for upsetting one of the stars and make him do just the opposite. Both parties usually referred to him as "the damned manager." In fact, a transfer player said to him one year, "For the first month I was here, I thought your first name was "Damned" and your last name was "Manager."

But he stuck it out because he had to. He developed a sharp tongue and a cynical, sarcastic outlook. He was a better athlete than most of them yet they expected him to serve them. They'd call him "damned manager" but when test time came, they wanted to use his notes or come study with him. He couldn't believe how dumb some of them were. A large percentage never graduated. He did. He wasn't about to take all that crap and not get something out of it.

He pulled into a rest stop to freshen up and take a last look at the directions Reed had sent. As he pulled out and before he built up speed, he saw an inviting crossover with a sign that said "Official vehicles only." He slowed for an instant but drove on. He'd come too far to turn back now.

The restaurant wasn't hard to find. He was early. He parked over to one side of the parking lot under a tree and just sat in the car—waiting and watching. Soon they began to arrive. Age had taken its toll. Most were overweight. There was a lot of baldheads and white hair. They shouted at each other and slapped each other on the back. He thought he could recognize some of them. One fellow hoisted himself out of his car and walked toward the restaurant. He nodded at some of the others. Nobody shouted at him. He was short and very large—so large that his arms couldn't hang down but stuck out at about forty-five degrees as they followed the contour of his body. He figured the man would go over 300 pounds. "Good lord," he thought, "could that be Wayne?" He was the right height and his walk seemed to show through all the fat. Wayne had been their All-American. At 5'6", 215 he played nose guard on their patented 5-4 defense. He was as hard to move as a tree stump and as quick as a cat. He'd come to school poor from a little town in Mississippi. But by his sophomore year when it became evident just how good he was, the boosters began to shower him with gifts. All of a sudden he had plenty of money to spend and more new clothes than his dorm closet would hold. Someone said that he came to college in overalls and left in a tux.

And clothes, money, and a new car his senior year wasn't all he left college with. Jack Donaldson was a big booster from Jackson who owned a string of hardware stores. His four daughters all went to Tech. They were all cheerleaders and they all married football players. Jack's wedding gift was the same to all—a new hardware store to run. Trudy was the youngest and she had latched onto Wayne early on. They were married after his senior season.

He glanced at his watch. It was time to go in. He'd put if off as long as he could. As he was locking his car, he heard someone yelling, "Larry! Larry!" He turned to see two men hurrying his way. One was Stan, a fullback, and the other was Eddie an end. Stan got there first and began to shake his hand. "Man, Larry, it's great to see you after all these years.

You remember Eddie here."

"Sure do," he answered, "Left End, number 84." They shook hands.

"You always had a good memory," said Eddie.

"When you put out jerseys every day, you get to know the numbers," he responded modestly.

As they walked to the door, Stan continued to talk. "You know, Larry, I wanna tell you something. I know I never said it when we were in school but Stan and I were talking about it on the way over here. You know, you were a damned good manager and we appreciate it."

"W-w-why thank you," stammered Larry, taken aback by the compliment.

"Yeah. And most of the fellows feel the same way," chimed in Eddie.

"That's great to hear," Larry replied. "Perhaps the luncheon wouldn't be too bad after all," he thought to himself.

Reed met them at the door with a money pouch in his hand. He grabbed Larry's hand and pumped it and slapped him on the back. "I knew if I kept at it, I'd get you back," he said. There was sincerity in his voice. "I've told everybody you'd be coming. That'll be fifteen dollars, fellows. That includes the tip. There's a cash bar in the corner." The three reached into their pockets. "Not for you, Larry," Reed continued. "Your first time back's on me."

"Thanks," Larry replied, "but I didn't intend to come as a charity case."

"You're not. I just wanna say 'Thanks.' Y'all go on back."

As they entered the dining room, Larry noted several clusters of men standing about with drinks in their hands, talking loudly. "Reliving past heroics,' Larry thought. It reminded him of the line in the country song, "The older I get, the better I used to be." The fat guy he'd pegged as Wayne was standing at the corner of the bar by himself.

"Well, look who's here." He looked up and recognized Red, a big tackle. Red was white now and much bigger. They shook hands. "Man, you look good. Have you put on any weight since college?"

He had put on about twenty pounds but he prided himself on staying fit. When new developments came along in surgery, he'd gotten his knee fixed. He still played tennis twice a week and ran in a few 10K races every year. Not too bad for a 74-year old. "Oh, I've added a few pounds," he answered. Say, is that Wayne standing over there by the bar?"

"Yep. That's him. I guess he must have gotten his bankruptcy settled. He's buying his own drinks this year."

"Now, is that any way to talk about our all-American?" Larry asked kiddingly.

"Yeah. He was an All-American one year in college but he's been an All-American ass hole for fifty." There was a sharpness in Red's voice that made Larry drop the topic.

Others began to drift by to speak to him. Many reminded him of things he'd done for them during their playing days—things he'd mostly forgotten. Wes, a halfback asked, "Did you ever get to a game when you hadn't packed something you needed?"

"Not that I can recall," responded Larry.

"I'm sure not," Wes replied. "You remember that night over in Little Rock I tore the whole sole off my shoe and you had me back on the field in a new pair before that series was over? And they were the right size, too. And while you were doing it, Coach Rich was standing there dog cussing you because my shoe tore up."

Larry did, indeed, remember that night and the others like it and he felt his stomach tighten. Coach Rich's reaction to any equipment failure was to cuss the manager. To Wes he replied, "That wasn't too hard. I always packed one extra pair of each size."

As they were talking, Larry noticed that George who'd played center didn't have a drink. "Come on, George. I'll buy you a drink," he said moving toward the bar.

"Can't," responded George. "You go ahead. I'm an alcoholic. Have to stay away from the sauce. But I've been sober for over ten years now."

Larry started to apologize but George just brushed it off. "No problem. You didn't know."

"But I'm not and I can," broke in Pete who'd been a linebacker and had played several years with the New York Giants after college. "Come on, but your money's no good. This is on me." He wouldn't even listen to Larry's protests.

He ordered a bourbon and moved over to Wayne who had a drink in his right hand and another sitting on the bar. He stuck out his hand. "Hello, Wayne."

Even Wayne's face was fat, his eyes almost lost among the mounds of flesh. They peered out at Larry for a long moment. Finally, the mouth spoke. "I don't sit my drink down to shake with nobody. I heard you were coming back this year." The hand raised the glass to the mouth.

"So much for being cordial," thought Larry as he dropped his hand, took his drink from the bartender, and moved away with Pete.

In a few steps, they bumped into Steve, another halfback, who greeted him warmly and then asked, "You remember that day we stripped you down?"

How could he forget something like that? It was a tradition that at one practice during each season, the whole team would pounce on one of the managers, strip him down to his jock strap and shoes, and send him back to the field house. It was snowing on his day. He was rounding up the balls at the end of practice when he heard shouts of "Get Larry!" He gave them a run for their money but they finally corned him. He didn't remember the cold so much as the embarrassment as he ran down by the main street with cars honking at him. "Sure I do," he replied icily.

"Well, I know this is a long time after the fact but I want to apologize for it. I don't know why we were so stupid and treated y'all like that."

Larry was stunned. It was the last thing he'd expected. Before he could speak, Pete broke in. "Did anyone ever tell you what Coach Rich said about it?" Larry shook his head. "Well, I couldn't chase you because I had a hurt leg and I was standing over by the coaches when it happened. You were running all over that field faking out all those folks and they were falling down all over the place in the snow. I didn't think they were ever going to catch you. One of the coaches said to Coach Rich, 'That boy can run. We ought to suit him up.' And Coach Rich said, 'I'm not about to put a uniform on a damned manager.' He sounded mad for some reason."

"He probably was," replied Larry. "He got mad when I got hurt in high school and I don't guess he ever got over it."

All conversation was brought to a halt by Reed banging on a glass with a knife for attention. "Okay, fellows. No long speeches. We're glad you're all back for another year. Larry's back for the first time and we're glad to have him." There was applause. "The salad bar is ready. Tell the waitresses what you want to drink. The bar will stay open. When you get through with the salads, the hot line will be ready and desserts after that. Find you name plates for seating. Now, let's have a prayer for this good food and thank the Good Lord for giving us another year. Reed offered a good prayer—not nearly as long and preachy as Larry thought it might be.

Everyone went to the salad bar—everyone except Wayne who stayed at the bar, drinking. Larry was looking for his place card when he saw two fellows waving him over to their table. He recognized Jim, a quarterback, and Ross, defensive back. Neither had played on the varsity. They had been perennial members of what today is called the "Scout" team, the team that runs the next opponent's plays against the varsity. At Tech in the '50s they'd been called "Scabeanies," "Scabs," or "Beanies." They seemed glad to see him.

At his place was a loose-leaf binder with the school logo on the cover. "What's this?" he asked.

"That's information on everybody," Ross answered. "We've all got one. We'll take your info home and put it in our books. Reed likes to do things right." It was then that Larry noticed that there was a copy of his information at everybody's place.

"That's nice," he said as he flipped the book open and saw that it included pictures of all their teams with seasons' records. "That's real nice."

He glanced to see who their other table mate was. His heart sank when he saw Wayne's name. "I see we'll be dining with our All-American," he said.

"Yeah," responded Ross, "get ready for a fun time. But looks like he's lost." With a plate of salad in one hand and a drink in the other, Wayne was wandering around on the other side of the dining room looking for his place. "Reckon we ought to holler at him?"

"Naw. Let him look," said Jim. "Even lab rats figure out the maze eventually."

"Looks like it might take him until next week sometime," said Ross. They both laughed.

"You both look good," commented Larry. "Tell me what you've been doing for the last fifty years. I know I could read about it in my book but I'd like to hear it from y'all.

"Well," began Jim, after a hitch in the Air Force I used the G. I. Bill, worked, got some loans, and made it through law school. Another fellow and I started a firm that's got about twenty attorneys now. I still go in a couple days a week as sort of a consultant. I've had a good career.

"That's great," said Larry.

About that time Wayne showed up but he didn't sit down. Instead he yelled loudly, "Reed! What the hell do you mean? I'm an All-American and you've got me sitting with two Beanies and a damned manager."

A voice came out of the crowd, "Sit your ass down. You're lucky you're not out in the parking lot." Wayne scanned the crowd with his little pig eyes but could not locate the culprit.

Reed came rushing over. "Now, Wayne, you know I move the seats around every year so we can visit with different folks. Next year I'll be sure to put you with some boys who're more of your caliber. Please don't make a scene." Larry detected a note of facetiousness in his voice.

Wayne just grunted before setting his salad and drink down and gingerly positioning his oversize butt on the too small chair. His salad filled a whole dinner plate and was covered with so much dressing that it was dripping off on one side. He didn't speak to his table mates but began to shovel his salad into his mouth, drizzling dressing down the front of his shirt. Occasionally, he would blot his shirtfront with his napkin.

Larry thought he ought at least to try to make polite conversation. "How've you been doing, Wayne?"

"Just great." Wayne replied. "Especially since I got that last bankruptcy settled."

"Last?" queried Larry.

"Yeah, I've had a great business career. Gone bankrupt three times." There was pride in his voice.

"Isn't that a little excessive?"

"Naw, that's no problem if you just remember one important thing—<u>never</u> go bankrupt with your own money." He reared back and laughed loudly. Dressing ran down his chin and dripped on his shirt.

"How's Trudy been?" asked Larry.

"Oh, she died about ten months ago. Cancer got her," Wayne said matter-of-factly.

"I'm sorry. I didn't know."

Wayne waved off his condolences. "It was for the best. She wasn't really living the way she was. Anyway, I got her inheritance and a new honey now."

"You got married again?" asked Jim.

"Naw. I guess you could call her my 'companion' if you know what I mean. She's about forty and a real looker. She gives me what I want and I give her what I want her to have and there are no strings attached. You boys ought to try it. It's a real good arrangement." The three just looked at each other without comment.

Wayne seemed to notice Larry's data sheet for the first time. He wiped off the spots of dressing and began to examine it. Larry turned to Ross. "Well, tell me what you've been up to for the last half century."

"Well, I served my two years of active duty in the Army and then went into coaching and teaching. I went back and got my Masters in administration and ended up as the principal of a middle school here in Memphis for about twenty years before I retired."

Wayne broke in, "Damn, Larry. Your data sheet's three pages long. Mine's only one page."

"Maybe you should have included your bankruptcies," observed Larry dryly. "They could have made a page or so." Jim and Ross chuckled behind their napkins. Wayne looked as if he were trying to figure out if he were being insulted. The three went for the main course leaving Wayne to finish his salad.

As they were reseating themselves, Larry asked Jim, "Say, did you ever get your shoulder fixed? It was coming out on a regular basis there toward the end."

"Yep. Sure did. After I started my practice and made a little money."

"I always wondered why Coach Rich didn't send you to get it fixed," said Larry. "After all, playing for him got it messed up in the first place."

"Shoot!" exclaimed Jim. "He wasn't about to spend money on a Beanie he knew would never play on the varsity. And he knew I had to keep my scholarship to stay in school. Anyway, when I asked him about it, he said to me, 'It's not your throwing arm. You'll be all right.'"

"Man, what an ass hole," commented Ross.

Wayne returned with a plate stacked up about three layers deep with slices of roast beef lapping over the side. He attached it with the gusto of a hound dog as he continued to examine Larry's data sheet.

"But you helped my shoulder when you got me those cantilever lineman pads. It didn't get knocked down nearly as much after that. Of course, I thought we were both going to get into trouble when Coach Leon saw me putting them on one day and hauled me down to the equipment room to get them changed. You member that?"

"Good Lord," Wayne broke in. "You've been to five colleges."

"Yes. That's right," Larry confirmed. And then to Jim, "I sure do. He was determined to get you back into some of those light back pads. They were about the sorriest excuse for a shoulder pad we had."

"You told him they were all broken and had been sent for repair," Jim continued. "I knew you had some but he couldn't find any when he looked through the equipment room."

"When I hid something in my equipment room, nobody found it." They both laughed.

"Damnation, you've got three degrees and one's a Ph.D." Wayne broke in again.

"Yes, you're still correct."

"You may have had a bum shoulder," said Ross, "but it didn't take you any time to learn the offense of every team we played and run it against the varsity each week. How in the dickens did you do that?"

"Oh, I don't know," replied Jim modestly. "I was always a quick study on that kind of stuff."

"Which team was the hardest?" asked Larry.

"Tennessee. I always hated that week. They were still running the single wing. It was totally different from anything else."

"And you were a college professor!" Wayne was back. "And a Dean!" Damn, I knew you were sort of smart but not <u>that</u> smart."

"Well, now you know," said Ross before turning to Larry. "You remember that day I screwed up tackling and Coach Rich sent me up on the hill to tackle that swinging tackling dummy for the rest of the day and he sent you with me to steady the dummy?"

"I sure do. That wasn't a good day for either one of us."

"It didn't take long until I was exhausted. And when he didn't hear that pulley squeak often enough, he'd yell at me to step it up. And when he caught you giving me some water, I thought he was going to kill both of us."

"Man, I <u>sure</u> remember that."

"Say, where'd you get that water? Coach Rich never would let us have any on the field."

"I always had a little in my coveralls in case we had to wash out any eye or a cut. I just thought you needed it. In fact, I thought you were about to pass out and I didn't want to have to carry you all the way to the field house."

"So you were really just thinking about yourself."

"That's right." They both laughed.

Wayne flipped over to the second page of Larry's data sheet and his eyes widened in surprise. "Good Lord! Did you write all these books?"

"Yes. I'm afraid I did."

"You sure had a lot to say," Wayne continued. "What are all these?" he asked as punched the page with his forefinger.

"Those are articles in historical journals," Larry explained.

"Damnation. I never knew anybody who could write stuff."

"Why are we not surprised?" asked Jim. Wayne's face screwed up as he tried to figure out if he were being put down.

Larry turned to Ross. "Say, you didn't play your senior year, did you?"

"Naw. That tackling dummy incident was part of it. You know back then when you got a four-year scholarship that meant four years. If you kept your nose clean and did what they told you to do, they had to keep you on. But if you quit, that was it. And Coach Rich wanted to have our scholarships back so he tried to runs some of us off. He gave us to that student coach after practice. You remember him."

"Yeah," replied Larry. "I believe it was Coach Alton."

"That's right. I've been trying to forget him ever since. Anyway, he'd take us down on the lower practice field and make us run wind sprints and do grass drills until I thought we'd all die. In fact, I thought Charlie <u>was</u> going to die one afternoon. We had to help him to the field house and that bastard Alton wouldn't even let the trainer see about him. Sometime he'd keep us so late we'd miss supper at the training table. Some just walked away and never came back. I had to have my scholarship to graduate but I knew I couldn't take another year of that. So, I just went to Coach Rich and told him so. He sat there at his desk and looked at me a long time and then he said, "Okay, you're right. I do want your scholarship. So I'll make a deal with you. You give me the scholarship and I'll keep you off the books.' He was an ass hole but he kept his word on that one. All my fees were paid and I got a meal book to eat at the main cafeteria. And there was never any problem with how much I ate. All I had to do was turn in the old book of stubs and get a new one."

"That's amazing," said Larry. "Was anybody else off the books like you?"

"Oh, I think there were a few more but we were told not to talk about it and we didn't."

Ross broke in. "You know, Larry, a lot of the fellows said you kept everything in your head. How true was that?"

"Well, I did keep some things in my head but not everything."

"Shoe size?"

"Yes, I guess I did know about everybody's shoe size."

"What was mine?"

Larry thought for a minute. "I think yours was a 10E and you wore a 36 long pant."

"That's right," said Ross in amazement.

"What about me?" asked Jim.

"Well, I think yours was a 9 1/2 D and your pant was a 32 regular."

"Amazing," said Jim.

Wayne had finished going over Larry's data sheet, so he folded it up and put it in his pocket. "Can I get in on this size game?"

"I suppose," said Larry. 'You've got a wide foot, 10 ½EEE as I recall and you wore a 39 short pant." Wayne just shrugged his shoulders.

Somebody said you knew everyone's locker combination, too, " said Ross.

"Oh, no. But I did know a few of the easy ones. I think yours was 0-10-20—easy to remember. Jim, I don't remember yours."

"What about mine?" asked Wayne. "Surely you remember the All-American's combination."

"Not really. I never had to open yours. You'd come in the first day, open it, lock the lock back, and throw it down in the bottom of your locker. You didn't even know your combination." Jim and Ross laughed.

This seemed to annoy Wayne. He began to look around his place as if he'd lost something. Finally, he said in a voice loud enough to be heard several tables away. "Damn, I'm outta bread. Manager, go get me a couple of rolls."

Everything got real quiet. Larry looked at him for a long moment realizing that he was serious. He forced himself to speak in a calm, measured voice. "I took a lot of your shit fifty years ago because I had no choice. Now I do. Go get your own damn rolls."

Anger boiled up in Wayne. He heaved himself to his feet.

"I'm an All-American. Managers do what I say. Let's go outside and settle this."

Larry looked at the hulk across the table, breathless from the exertion of rising from his chair. Just for an instant he was tempted to take the challenge, go outside, and humiliate Wayne in front of everyone. But he controlled the urge and spoke quietly. "Why don't you sit your ass down, Wayne, before you really embarrass yourself."

Wayne got angrier and his voice got louder. "Yeah, you really think you're something. You come back here with college degrees and a bunch of books and make fun of me. Hell, I was All-American. You were nothing but a damned manager." He then turned to address the rest of the diners. "I been coming back every year but if this guy comes back again, don't look for me. I'm outta here."

As he stalked from the room, comments were shouted at him from all directions. "Aren't you gonna stay and eat three desserts like you usually do?" "Does this mean we can cancel our order for the oversized chair?" Wayne shouted obscenities at them all until the door slammed behind him.

For a moment or two there was silence and then the old players began to get up and come by Larry's table to apologize for Wayne and to tell him just how much they wanted him to come back. Reed sat down in Wayne's vacated chair. "I'm just gonna call Wayne and tell him he's not welcome anymore."

"Please don't do that," Larry responded. "I didn't come back to cause problems. It'll be easier for me to stay away."

Reed wouldn't hear of that solution. "Let's wait a while before we decide." And that's the way they left it.

The rest of the meal was rather subdued. The men talked in hushed tones. The good-natured kidding and boisterous laughter was over. Finally, Reed stood up, thanked everyone for coming, gave the date for next year's gathering, and said he hoped everyone would come back. He looked directly at Larry when he said "everyone." "Yeses" came from all over the room.

As he walked out with several people, Larry saw that everyone had stopped on the sidewalk. He soon saw why. Wayne had not gotten far. He was sitting on a bench under a dogwood tree. He was slumped forward with his head in his hands holding a white handkerchief to his face. It was obvious he was crying. His former teammates stood around in embarrassment, shuffling their feet. No one seemed to know what to do or even if they should do anything. Finally, someone asked, "Shouldn't we try to help him?"

Baker, the tackle who had played next to Wayne replied, "I've been trying to help the sombitch for fifty years. It's somebody else's turn. I'm going home." With that he headed for the parking lot. A few followed.

For some reason he could not fathom, Larry walked over and sat down on the bench next to Wayne. When he peeked out of his hands and saw who it was, he began to sob audibly. Larry placed his arm across Wayne's shoulder and realized he was saying something. He leaned close and heard, "I'm so sorry Larry. I'm so sorry, I'm so sorry…."

Larry patted him on the shoulder and said, "I'll see you next year, champ."

15
THE SWAMP

Zula May was walking through the cornfield. It was sometime about middle of the morning but it was already hot and the tall stalks prevented any cooling breeze from reaching her—even if there had been one. Sweat pasted her faded housedress to her body and she wiped the droplets from her brow before they could sting her eyes. Sim and Caleb didn't want her to go. "Jest leave things be," Sim had said. They were plowing out the cotton on the other side of the place and wouldn't come to the house until dinner. The dinner food was about ready. She'd left it simmering in pots on the back part of the wood cook stove. She'd be back before them. They'd never know she'd been gone.

She could smell it before she saw it. Its aroma laid heavy in the nostrils. It was more mysterious than offensive. Emerging from the corn, Zula May stopped in the shade of a giant cypress and gazed into The Swamp. She came here often—too often for her sons. "Leave things be, Ma; leave things be." Their words would not leave her. She'd tried. She really had. But they didn't know of the early years. She tried to think about those when she came here—tried to think about Pleg and those few good years. It seemed she was closer to him when she could see and smell and feel The Swamp.

The Swamp was large. She didn't know exactly how large. Folks said it stretched all the way to the river and no telling how far up and down its banks. She just knew it was big—big enough to get lost in and stay lost. The water was a brackish brown that hid everything more than two or three inches below its surface. The Spanish moss hung low over the water. Little sunlight penetrated the thick cypress canopy leaving the area in a perpetual twilight even in the middle of the day. Some folks said black panthers still lived there but she'd never seen one. She did know there were gators and loggerhead snapping turtles and cottonmouths. She'd seen those. Folks also said there was quick sand in places that would suck a man to his death beneath the brown water and leave no trace he was ever there. Most people saw the Swamp's sinister side and feared it. Zula May saw it as a place of refuge.

The water rippled as a snake made its way across a small patch of open water. Zula May's thoughts turned to those early years. She was 16 and Pleg was good to her—even tender at times. They both worked hard to wrest the new-ground farm from the underbrush and stumps left by the logging company.

But then, things changed. The boys came along followed in a few years by the Depression. Cotton prices went down and stayed down. To make ends meet, Pleg started running a trap line in The Swamp. A splashing startled her. She peered into the gloom and just for instant she thought she saw him striding out of the dimness with his gum boots on and the mink and muskrat from his traps thrown over his shoulders. Reality returned quickly. She knew he'd been in The Swamp too long. He'd never come out.

She tried to stop her mind from thinking any further but she was powerless to do so. Her brain was like a runaway team of mules, impossible to turn or stop. She remembered the pointed finger, the nasty words, the curses, the accusations that she and the boys were dragging him down, the first jug of shine, the fists. She could still feel the pain from the blows. She rubbed her face as if to rub the old hurts away and began to cry—not for herself but for Pleg. Pleg only beat her when he was drinking and since she had no place to go, she had determined to endure it. But the night he beat her boys with a doubled-up piece of plow line, The Swamp became their refuge. She'd let him get drunk enough before she and her sons would slip away. He'd be too drunk to find them in the dark so he'd attack the house breaking furniture and kicking holes in the walls.

After he'd sober up, he was always sorry and would try to nail things back together. He'd promise not to do it anymore—and he wouldn't until another jug of shine would show up. Zula May couldn't remember how many years this went on—didn't want to remember really. She just knew it was too many. But she did remember the last time. The thought of that night made her shiver in spite of the July heat. She shoved that memory away.

A blue heron walked out from behind a cypress knee and right up to her and cocked his head to one side like he was asking her a question—just like the sheriff had that day. He'd just walked up on the porch late one afternoon after the boys had come in from the field. He had a deputy with him. Zula May's heart sank as she answered his knock. They removed their hats. "Evening, Miz Hankins," said the Sheriff.

"Evening, Sheriff,"

"I believe you know Ike here."

"Yes. Yes I do. Evening, Ike."

"Evening, ma'am."

"Y'all are jest in time fer supper. Would you be staying? We got plenty."

"No ma'am, we can't. We's on bizness. Is Pleg around?"

Zula May thought her heart would pound its way out of her chest. "No. No, he's not," she answered.

"What about the boys?"

"There're here. They're doing the chores. I'll git 'em. Won't y'all come on in?" The men followed her through the house to the kitchen where she offered them seats in two straight chairs. As she went out the back door, Caleb was just coming in from the barn. Sim was at the woodpile splitting stove wood. She could not bear to see him use the axe so she closed her eyes and turned her head to one side before calling out, "Come on in, boys, we got company."

When they'd all found seats around the kitchen, the Sheriff began. "Ain't nobody seen Pleg around for quite some time. They's rumors about that there might have been some foul play. Does y'all know where Pleg is?"

The three Hankins exchanged glances. Zula May drew in her breath to speak but Sim spoke first. "He's in The Swamp."

The Sheriff was surprised by Sim's frankness. "You mean he's in The Swamp running his trap line and he'll be to the house directly?"

"No, sir," Sim replied. "He's been in The Swamp going on two months now. We figure he won't be coming back."

"You mean he's lost in The Swamp?"

"That's what we figure."

The Sheriff almost couldn't believe what he was hearing. "And y'all didn't tell nobody, didn't git no help to look fer him?"

"Wasn't no need, Sheriff. You ever know of anybody that's been lost in there that's ever been found?" Sim said matter-of-factly.

"No. No, I guess not. But how could Pleg of all people git lost in there? He's been running a trap line in there for years."

Caleb spoke for the first time. "Darkness and shine kin make a person do crazy things, Sheriff."

"Shine?" queried the sheriff.

"'At's right," responded Caleb. "It wuz jest after gud dark when he went in with a jug of shine."

"Did y'all hunt fer 'em?" asked the sheriff.

Warn't no need," answered Sim. "We figured after 'bout two days that we wuzn't gonna find him noway. Figured he fell inna deep hole and drownded or maybe a gator got 'im." Zula May winced at the thought. "Anyway, we had to finish plantin' the late corn."

"And none of y'all never told nobody?" asked the sheriff incredulously

"Didn't see no need to," responded Sim.

"Did he take anything with him, clothes or anything?"

"No. Jest what he had on—and the jug of shine," answered Caleb.

"Mind if I look around a little, Miz Hankins?"

"No. Jest hep yourself, Sheriff," answered Zula May.

As he got to his feet the sheriff observed, "I don't believe I've ever seen a cleaner kitchen. Hit looks like hit's been fresh scrubbed."

"We may not have much, Sheriff, but we try to be clean," responded Zula May nervously wiping her hands on her apron.

She showed the sheriff the front room where the boys slept and the room across the dogtrot that was hers and Pleg's. "Your furniture is sure in bad shape," observed the sheriff.

"We're gonna get some better if cotton prices are good this fall," volunteered Sim.

"Where's Pleg's stuff?" asked the sheriff.

"Rat thar in the chiffer robe," answered Zula May. "Top two drawers and right hand door."

The drawers contained some socks and several pairs of underwear. The mirror had been broken out of the door and its hinges bent so that it wouldn't stay closed. Three pairs of overalls and four work shirts, all starched and pressed, hung on hangers. A pair of gum boots and a pair of high-top work shoes sat on the floor. A straw hat was perched on the top.

"If he does come back, his clothes is ready," said Zula May. Her voice was noticeably shaky.

"So I see," mused the sheriff. "But why would he go to The Swamp, drunk or sober, without his boots?"

The three Hankins exchanged glances again. "He had on

his old ones," volunteered Sim.

The sheriff did not respond. He just stood for a moment rubbing his chin in deep thought.

After poking around for another minute or two, the two officers took their leave. Zula May ushered them out. She closed the screen door and leaned against the wall beside it, wiping her face on her apron. She heard Ike say as the two paused at the top of the porch steps, "Well, you know Peck Henson says he sold Pleg a half-gallon of shine 'bout that time."

"Yes, that's right," responded the sheriff. "But there's one thing that really bothers me."

"What's that?" asked the deputy.

"Have you ever known a man as pore a Pleg Hankins to have two pairs of boots?"

"No. Can't say as I have," replied Ike. The men walked down the steps and out of earshot.

Zula May watched two soft-shelled turtles jockey for position on a dead snag by The Swamp's edge as they sunned themselves. She tried to concentrate on the turtles so that the memory of that last night wouldn't come back. It worked for a few seconds but the memory won—just like it always did.

She knew Pleg had left the field early that afternoon which was not a good sign. She hoped it wasn't happening again—but she knew deep down that it was. Sim and Caleb had come in from the field and were doing the chores. She was finishing up supper when she heard Pleg come up on the back porch and kick off his work shoes. He washed up in the pan on the wash shelf, threw the dirty water into the backyard, and came into the kitchen. She turned around as he sat down at his place and put the half-gallon jug down on the table with a thud. "Do you have to do that, Pleg?" she asked pleadingly.

"Yes I do, woman." There was a nasty tone in his voice. "I deserve some pleasure outta life and y'all don't gimmie none." She noted that the jug was not full. He'd started on the way home.

She went out on the back porch and pretended to wash her hands. Caleb was still at the barn. Sim was splitting stove wood. Zula May walked out to the woodpile. Sim was good with the axe. He wielded it like a surgeon's scalpel as he split the white oak into small pieces. He had to have seen Pleg come in with the jug. Sim's jaw was set hard. Their eyes met. She started to speak but Sim cut her off. "We ain't going to The Swamp no more, Ma."

"What . . ." was all she got out before he cut her off again. "I said we ain't going to The Swamp no more." There was an edge to his voice she'd never heard before. The wood flew off his axe in a blur. She knew he had just turned sixteen and thought himself a man. He could do a man's work. But Pleg was a man—even when drunk. She turned and walked back to the house dreading the impending confrontation.

Tension hung heavy over the supper table. Pleg drank from the jug as he ate. "You boys git finished plowing out the corn?" he asked.

"'Bout an hour left," answered Sim.

"Why didn't you stay and finish?"

"Had to come in and git the chores done," retorted Sim.

"Well, git that done first thing in the morning and then start chopping the cotton," directed Pleg.

"We intend to," replied Sim as he got to his feet. "Gotta go to the toilet."

"Can't it wait 'til after supper?' asked Pleg.

"Naw, it can't," said Sim as he stalked out letting the screen door slam behind him.

"'At boy's 'bout to git too big fer his britches," stated Pleg as he took a swig from the jug and wiped his mouth with the back of his hand.

In a few minutes, Sim came back but stopped just inside the door behind Pleg. "Git yore ass back to the table, boy, and finish yore supper," Pleg ordered.

Zula May looked up. The forkful of cabbage stopped half way to her open mouth as she saw the yellow light from the coal oil lamp reflect off the cold steel of the double-bit axe. Zula May closed her eyes.

16
THE BROUSSARD BOYS

Most every community seems to have its share of ne'er-do-wells—those folk who for generations have operated outside of both the prevailing community standards and the law and, as a result, have always attracted an inordinate amount of attention from local law enforcement agencies. So it is that deep southwest Louisiana and extreme southeast Texas is the home of one of these miscreant clans—the Broussards.

Two of the Broussard boys were on the prowl. They were first cousins, Boudireaux and Boudineaux, who had been born within a week of each other. Their mothers had both hoped for twins, which accounted for their names. They had grown up together and looked so much alike most folks outside their closest family members thought that they were.

It was well past midnight and they had been thrown out of two local roadhouses that evening for boosting beers. Since they had no money, they would go into a roadhouse and mingle with the crowd. Usually one would distract a customer while the other would boost his long neck leaving an empty bottle in its place. They tried to pick a drinker who maybe had had a few too many and was easily confused. They would then amble off into the crowd and share their ill-gotten refreshment.

Sometimes they might just brazenly walk by and pick up a customer's beer when he headed for the restroom. This method was more easily detected but one long neck looks about like another one and unless someone pointed a finger, they were home free.

On this particular night, the bartenders and customers had been more vigilant than usual resulting in the Broussards not having consumed nearly as much beer as they wanted. And not having enough gas to drive to a more distant nightspot, the cousins were trying to figure out what to do with the rest of the evening when Boudireaux said, "You know wot would tas' good to youself, Cousin Boudineaux? A roas'd pig. We could put him over top a hot fire an' turn himself round an' round until he jes' right for ourselfs to eat."

To this suggestion Boudineaux replied, "Hush up that talk out of yo' mouth. You know we got no pig. We done eat all our animals 'cept for two cats. Where you think we gonna got a pig?"

But, being the thinker he was, Boudireaux had that all figured out. "From ol' Thibodaux's place. It's only 'bout three-two miles from here. He got plenty hogs in that big lot 'side de road an' dey all layin' round 'sleep. I jes step 'cross de fence an' pick ourselfs up a nice roas'in pig an' lay himself in de back of this pick-me-up truck an' 'way we go."

That sounded good to Boudineaux, so they hulled out for Thibodaux's farm. When they got close, Boudineaux cut off the one headlight and coasted to a stop beside the hog lot. Boudireaux jumped the fence and picked his way gingerly among the sleeping animals until he found a shoat the size he wanted. The pig hardly grunted when Boudireaux picked him up and carried him back to the fence where Boudineaux was waiting. He handed the pig to Boudineaux and then hopped over the fence only to find him just standing beside the truck holding the pig. "What for you waiting, Cousin Boudineaux? Lay him in de truck an' les go!"

"You dumb Cajun!" Boudineaux replied. "This truck got no tailgate! An' anyhow de 'sides so low he could jump himself out anytime he want."

But, the quick thinking Boudireaux came up with a solution. "Jes lay him in de floorboard up front. He mos' still 'sleep. He be jes' fine."

Boudineaux did so and found that his cousin was right. The pig grunted a few times and seemed to go into a deep slumber when the truck started moving.

The two cousins headed for home with their ill-gotten prize. Both could almost taste the roast pork that would be the end product of the night's foray. However, they had not counted on the vigilance of the local law enforcement folk.

Two deputies, Cletus and Dub, were out on patrol as they were most every night. They had pulled their car off into a small grove of trees behind a picnic table at a roadside park to take a break. They had not been there long when the Broussard cousins came by.

"Here comes a one-eyed car," observed Dub as the Broussards approached.

As the vehicle passed, Cletus added, "It's a truck. And no tail lights at all and I don't see a license plate either. The fenders look like they're tied on with bailing wire."

"It's got to be a Broussard truck," Dub concluded. "Wonder what they're up to this time of night? Let's go see." With that he started the patrol car's engine and fell in behind the Broussards. The deputies followed for a mile or so before turning on the flashing lights and hitting the siren a couple of times to pull the truck over.

As soon as the Broussards saw the lights behind them, they knew it had to be a patrol car. "Well, Cousin Smartass, wot we gonna do now? Maybe when they 'rest us, they put us in de same cell. That way I can pound you some on you smart head." Boudineaux was not too happy with his cousin.

But Boudireaux was not one to give up easily. The groggy pig and the darkness of the night gave him an idea. "Don't shook youself up, Cousin Boudineaux, I gonna sot this pig up 'tween us an' put my hat over top his head. Les' jam himself in good an' maybe they don't notice." This they did and then sat awaiting the approaching deputies.

Cletus and Dub approached the truck from either side. They shined their flashlights underneath, along the sides, and in the bed seeing nothing unusual. They stopped beside the windowless doors and threw their beams around the cab, even on the floorboard, but saw nothing amiss.

"You boys Broussards?" Cletus asked.

""Yessir." "Yessir."

"Well, y'all couldn't be up to anything good. You boys are either coming from doing something wrong or you're headed that way," Cletus continued.

"What'er you boys' names?" asked Dub as he shined his light into the face of the one on the passenger side.

"Boudineaux."

He moved his light to the face of the driver.

"Boudireaux."

Then, for the first time, Dub noticed what he thought was a person squshed up between the two and mostly hidden. Throwing a beam in the pig's face he demanded, "and yours?"

Boudireaux reacted by jabbing his right elbow sharply into the pig's ribs. A loud "Oink" came from the startled animal.

Cletus took over at this point. "We *could* run you boys in for light and tag violations. But we ain't gonna do that. The sheriff don't wanna fool with no Broussards 'less it's for something big. So, we're gonna let you boys go on home. If we see y'all again tonight, we're taking y'all to jail. Y'all understand me?"

"Yessir," came in unison from the truck's cab. The pig remained silent.

The deputies backed away giving the truck a last look with their flashlights as it moved down the road. They went back to their patrol car and continued their nightly duties.

Before they had gone many miles, Dub realized that something was wrong with Cletus. Any attempt at conversation was met with a simple "yep" or "nope." Even when asked two or three times what was wrong, Cletus' reply was, "Nothing."

Finally, Dub could stand it no longer. "Now listen here, Cletus, we've rode these back roads together for nigh on twenty years. One time you even saved my life and you know I'd do the same for you. Why, we even grew up playing ball together. And you married my sister. I *know* something's wrong and I wanna know what it is."

Cletus pulled the car to the side of the road and stopped before replying. “You’re right, Dub. We grew up playing ball together. I’m married to your sister. I guess we have rode together for nearly twenty years. And I saved your life once and I know you’d save mine. But, …I’ll tell you what’s the gospel truth. I do believe that Oink Broussard is the ugliest sonofabitch I have ever laid eyes on."

SQUAWK 7500

Terrorist Hijacking of Pacifica 762

Captain Mike Rendell started out his workday like all the workdays before – just another normal day of flying. After spending a raucous night partying with his crew, he and his first officer were looking forward to a nice relaxing flight to the West Coast.

"Flaps 1, climb power", Mike repeated as he responded to the command of Gary Ellis, his new-hire First Officer. Mike positioned the flap lever from the "5" spot to the "1" spot and retarded the thrust levers to approximately eighty-eight percent of full power. This was the standard "after take-off" configuration and gave the aircraft its' best rate of climb in relation to burning the least amount of fuel. Pacifica Airlines Flight 762 had just departed from Chicago's Midway Airport. On board the Boeing 737 were 137 passengers, three flight attendants, and two pilots.

However, it didn't take long for events to unfold that would thrust Captain Rendell and his crew into one of the most terror-filled days of their commercial airline careers. The lives of his flight attendants and his passengers hung in the balance as Mike battled the elements, a deranged passenger, and aircraft malfunctions as he attempted to bring his fully loaded jumbo jet in for a safe landing.

Author:	**Captain Steve A. Reeves**
Publishing House:	TotalRecall Publications, Inc.
Publication Date:	9/26/2008
ISBN Book:	978-1-59095-844-5
ISBN eBook:	978-1-59095-845-2

Coon Dogs and Outhouses
Volume I
Tall Tales From The Old South

This first collection of his stories is part remembrance of a culture that is gradually fading, part recollection of lessons learned over a lifetime. Luke Boyd's matter-of fact style and clarity of detail are cut from the cloth of the oral tradition, which flourished in the rural South of his upbringing. He deftly places the hilarious story of chain saw-toting Phinos Ledbetter and his botched baptism at the East Fork Southern Missionary Baptist Church alongside the powerful memory of an uncle known by the poor tenant farmhands he served only as "The Jesus Doctor."

The author's characters are depicted so clearly and accurately as to leave the reader guessing which stories are fact and which are imagined. And whether the teachers in these tales are smudged with the dust of chalk or caked with the mud of the field, their lives and lessons are faithfully recorded here in the straightforward prose of Luke Boyd.

Author:	**Lucas G. Boyd**
Publishing House:	TotalRecall Publications, Inc.
Publication Date:	9/1/2008
ISBN Book:	978-1-59095-837-7
ISBN eBook:	978-1-59095-838-4

www.ingramcontent.com/pod-product-compliance
Lightning Source LLC
Chambersburg PA
CBHW070506120726
47910CB00003B/1137

* 9 7 8 1 5 9 0 9 5 8 3 9 1 *